Ella and Micha:

Infinitely and Always

JESSICA SORENSEN

For information:

jessicasorensen.com

Cover Design and Photography: Mae I Design

http://www.maeidesign.com/

Ella and Micha: Infiintely and Always(The Secret)

ISBN: 978-1499583427

Ella and Micha: Infinitely and Always

Chapter 1
Micha

Encore! Encore! Encore!

Lights blind me from above as I step out onto the stage again and grasp the microphone stand. The background music throbs in my veins as I pour my soul out to a room full of a thousand strangers, all begging me to understand them, see them, connect with them.

Love, it's always there.
Aching, hard to bear.
Burning inside my veins.
Heart filled sorrow, igniting pain.
Shattered. Your words cut deep.
Strike my soul and let me weep.

It's not really my soul that I speak of anymore. A long time ago, yes, back when love was hard to endure. Back when it was one-sided. If I were to write a song about how I feel now, it'd end up sounding like one of those frilly, pop ones. I'm too happy now. At least, that's what my producers have been saying lately.

Too happy?

Is that even a thing?

Apparently it is because it's been repeated a lot. I'm not sure what they expect me to do. Become less happy?

Yeah, even if that was possible, which it's not, I wouldn't do it. All of my pre-Ella years—the less happy life they speak of—is something I'd never go back to. Her and our happiness is the most important thing to me.

"Thank you, everyone," I say into the microphone as I finish up the song. Then I collect my guitar and stride off the stage, dodging around the next band.

I usually linger around and sign a few autographs, but there's something important waiting for me in the back room. Plus, my heart hasn't really been into signing lately. I'm not sure why exactly; whether the pressure to change is starting to get to me, or if I'm just exhausted.

At twenty-five years old, I've been playing for the same record label for a few years now. I have put out three albums, been on fifteen tours, have written so many songs I've lost track, and sometimes, I miss playing just for me.

As my thoughts and worries weigh at my mind, I practically sprint down the dimly lit hallway and past a father and young son, who are waiting in front of one of the doors. Who knows why the dude has a kid back here, but it reminds me of another thing I'm missing out on.

Starting a family.

But, there's more to that than just being on the road. Ella has made it pretty clear she's not ready to be a mother—might never be. The last thing I'd ever do is pressure her into that, but as our extended family grows, I find myself wishing for a child of my own more and more.

Lost in my thoughts, I reach the closed door at the end of the hall. As I reach for the knob, I'm side-blocked by my producer, Mike Anderly. I try not to curse under my breath, but it's difficult. I don't want to talk business tonight. I want to get behind that damn door and to my serenity I haven't had in over a month.

"Great job, Micha." He sticks out his hand to shake.

I shake his hand and offer him a curt smile. "Thanks."

He fake smiles back, a new routine of ours. "I just wanted to know if you have thought anymore about the tour and the new album."

"A little." I switch my guitar into my other hand and then scratch the back of my neck. "Look, I'm not sure if it's the right direction for me to go. I like singing my own songs, and the whole sexy, manwhore singer thing... Well, I really don't want it to be my thing."

"There are a lot worse things than that, Micha. So far, you've been really lucky in this business."

"I know that," I reply with a weighted sigh. "And I'm grateful for everything you've done for me, Mike, I really am, but... I'm just not feeling the new image."

"Look, Micha," he says, getting right down to business. "As much as I would love to tell you to keep going in the direction that you are, it's not really up to me. It's up to the label."

I frown. "So you're saying what, exactly? That, if I don't change, I lose the label?"

He shrugs. "Sorry, kid, but it's just how things are." His hard expression slightly softens. "Look, if it was up to me, I'd let you do whatever."

Yeah, right. I know Mike enough to understand how full of bullshit he is ninety-nine percent of the time.

He places a hand on my shoulder. "Just think about it, okay? You'll have a few weeks off coming up in the next couple of months. Go on a vacation or something. Clear your head a little."

I offer him the same fake smile he gave me earlier. "Fine."

"There ya go." He pats my cheek, pleased, as if I've just told him I agree with changing my image. Then he turns and walks away to charm whatever other bands he can find lurking around the hallways.

Me, I reach right for the doorknob, glad the tour will be over in two months because this shit is starting to get old.

As I push open the door and step into the small room, I force myself to shed all of my problems and leave them out in the hallway.

"Hey, sad boy," Ella greets me the moment I enter, wrapping her arms around me and pulling me close.

"*Sad boy?*" I drop my guitar to the floor and hug her back with everything I have in me. Suddenly, I can breathe freer. "I'm way beyond happy right now."

I haven't seen her in almost a month, and I didn't realize until now just how great of an affect her absence has on me. Ever since she opened her own art gallery and started traveling with me less, being on the road has gotten harder. It's been almost two years that I've been doing this on my own, and the loneliness has begun to take a toll on me.

"Yeah, but you weren't earlier." She nuzzles her nose into the crook of my neck. "You looked sad playing tonight."

"You could tell?" The intoxicating vanilla scent of her is almost enough to fade my problems away.

"Of course I could tell." She presses her lips to my throbbing pulse. "After five years of marriage, I know you as well as you know me, mister."

I chuckle as I pull away and drop a soft kiss to her full lips, her taste warming my body. "Is that so?"

Her beautiful green eyes sparkle. "Of course that's so. I'm always right. Haven't you realized that yet?"

Laughter slips from my lips as I cup her face between my hands. "I love you, pretty girl."

She smiles as I lean in to kiss her. "I love you, too."

Our lips meet halfway, and the connection sparks an overwhelming desire. My body becomes way too eager, way too fast. Within ten seconds, I'm unbuttoning her shirt, tugging at the locks of her auburn air, and tasting her with hunger, lust, love, and need.

She softly chuckles against my lips as I jerk her shirt off. "You're always so horny every time I visit."

"Mmmm." I suck her tongue into my mouth as I cup her ass and press her body into mine. "You taste so good."

When she runs her fingers through my hair and giggles, the sound is like soulful music to my ears.

"You're all sweaty from performing," she whispers against my lips while her hand wanders down my back, then she slips it into the back pocket of my jeans. "It's sexy."

With one swift movement and a low growl, I scoop her up into my arms and plant her ass on top of the table in the corner of the room. "You're the sexy one." I spread her legs and grind myself against her.

She moans in response, her head falling back, her eyelids fluttering. "God, that feels so good."

"It's about to feel even better," I murmur against her lips as my fingers wander to the clasp of her bra.

Right as I'm about to unfasten it, someone knocks at the door.

"Go away," I shout then devour Ella with my lips again as I unhook her bra and slip the straps from her shoulders. As the fabric falls from her chest, I plant needy kisses down her neck to the base of her throat, trailing down all the way to her breasts. Taking her nipple into my mouth, I suck hard, just how she likes it.

"Micha," she gasps, her knees coming up to my hips as her fingers tangle through my hair.

I move to the other nipple and wrap my lips around it, giving it the same treatment.

Knock. Knock. Knock.

"Micha, open the door. We need to talk," Mike calls out.

"In a minute," I shout back, growing frustrated because he's ruining the mood. And it's the only mood Ella and I are going to have for a while.

"I know Ella's in there," he says, "but I promised the house manager that you'd sign autographs for an hour, so you need to get out here. It's good for your image, too. It shows the fans you appreciate their support."

Letting out a frustrated grunt, my forehead falls against Ella's bare shoulder. "I don't want to sound ungrateful, but I'm really getting tired of this shit."

"Of what?" she asks, smoothing her hand over my head. "Of signing autographs?"

"No." Shaking my head, I stand up straight. "Mike, the label, my image."

Her bottom lip juts out, and it's so damn sexy I almost forget I'm upset. "I'm sorry, sweet boy. I don't ever want you to be unhappy."

"I'm not unhappy," I assure her. The last thing I want Ella to do is worry. "I'm just not sure—"

"Micha, get your ass out here." Mike bangs on the door and keeps banging.

"Fuck." I kiss Ella one last time then back up to the door. "Wait for me?"

"Of course," she responds, hopping off the table and reaching for her bra on the floor. "Where else would I go?"

Smiling, I open the door and walk out of the room. The smile vanishes from my face the moment I enter the hallway and leave the only person I really want to see behind. Because I only feel like myself when I'm with Ella—only

12

then do I feel whole—which leaves me wondering if maybe it's time to quit.

But then what? What would I be if I didn't have my music? A good husband. I'm not even sure if I am since I'm never home. I want to be home more. I want to be a great fucking husband, have a job I love and one where I can see my wife every day. I want to know my home. Take care of it. Start my own family.

I just wish I could get the guts to do it.

Chapter 2
Ella

Poor Micha. He looks so sad and has for quite a while. It nearly kills me to see him so depressed, especially since I know firsthand how dark depression can be. I still struggle with my own sadness here and there, particularly when I've been alone for too long. I've learned how to be strong, though, to support Micha and his dream like he's done for me.

"I need to find a way to help him," I mutter to myself as I sit at the dimly lit bar, drinking an ice-cold beer while waiting for Micha to finish up signing for the fans.

The bar is attached to the space where the concert took place. The area has been cleared out, most of the lights turned off, and the air is ghostly quiet. The silence is soothing to me along with the alcohol in my veins. I needed soothing tonight after a crazy fan tried to put me in my place on the way backstage. Micha has gotten enough publicity that the hardcore fans recognize me now.

"You're Micha Scott's wife, right?" she sneered as the bouncer moved aside to let me through.

Choosing to ignore her, I tucked my identification into

my back pocket and headed for the door.

"Excuse me. I'm talking to you." She reached over the roped area and grabbed my hair. Yes, actually freaking grabbed my hair!

When my head whipped in her direction and my hands balled into fists, she let me go.

"Touch me again, and that face of yours won't be so pretty anymore."

The bouncer stepped in then and shoved her back, but she made sure to get in her final words.

"He slept with me, you know!" she cried out as she stumbled back from the rope. "You're husband. And he fucking loved it. He loves me."

She was short and curvy with wavy blonde hair and wearing too much eye shadow. So not Micha's type.

Rolling my eyes, I slipped into the building and let the door slam shut behind me. I was pissed off. Irate. It's not like I believed her. I know Micha well enough to know he would never cheat on me. Plus, when I was on the road with him in the past, there were a lot of fans that said the same thing, even though I was with him. It's still a lot to take in sometimes, and there's a part of me—one I'll never tell Micha about—that wishes he'd find a way to leave the touring behind and be home with me more.

15

I love him enough not to say anything, though, not to crush his dream.

Despite all the drama tonight, it was still amazing to see him perform. I sometimes wonder how he does it, how he stands in front of a thousand rowdy fans, so at ease. Well, he used to be, anyway. Tonight, he seemed restless to get off the stage and much less eager than he normally is to sign autographs.

"You're Micha Scott's wife, right?" the dark haired, late twenties bartender interrupts my thoughts as she appears in front of me.

I hesitate. If I've learned anything over the last couple of years, it is that it's not necessarily a good thing in the female world to be the wife of a sexy rockstar. Hence, the crazy blonde tonight.

"Relax," she says as if sensing my edginess. "I swear I'm not some crazy fan. Just making sure you're not a customer, so I can lock up the bar."

"Oh." I nod then swallow the last gulp of beer. "Yeah, go ahead. I'm just waiting for him to…" I flick my hand in the air, searching for a word that would describe what Micha does. Even though I can't see him right now, I've observed enough signings that I can perfectly picture the dazzling smile he offers each person, both male and female.

"Quit charming everyone," the bartender finishes for me as she collects the empty beer bottle.

"Yeah, I guess that's kind of what he's doing." I thoughtfully smile as I glance over at the stage. All that's left of tonight's concert is a piano and two large speakers. A man wearing black pants and a T-shirt is closing the curtain, and the stage slowly slips from my view.

"You can hang around here if you want to," the bartender says as she pops the cap off another beer and sets the bottle opener down. "I'm sure it gets a little intense being around all those swoony females."

I raise my eyebrows and laugh. "Yeah, it kind of does."

She flips one of her dark locks off her shoulders then rests her arms on the counter. "I totally understand. I used to date this drummer, and I got some of the nastiest looks while we were going out. And sometimes, they'd even send me notes."

"Yeah, I've been there, too. In fact, for about two months last year, I kept getting threatening texts from someone who was clearly in love with Micha. We had to change my number, it got so bad. I wish they'd just chill out and focus on his music instead of him." Usually, I'm not so chatty, but I guess I'm lonelier than I thought.

"I hate to break it to you, but the more popular Micha gets, the worse it'll probably become," she says. When I frown, she adds, "Don't worry. All you have to do is ignore them. And trust your husband, too." She smiles as she offers me the beer. "Here, this one's on the house."

"Thanks." I oblige, taking the bottle from her, wondering if she's right. Will things get more intense the more popular Micha gets? If so, things are going to suck balls.

The bartender begins wiping the counters off while I sip on my beer and stare at the television screen. By the time the bartender says good-bye and heads out, telling me the owner of the bar will lock up after all the bands have cleared out, it's been almost two hours since I sat down.

Mike said Micha would only have to sign for one hour. Then again, Mike usually feeds Micha shit just so he'll be more cooperative.

I finish my beer, growing more restless with each minute that ticks by. Eventually, I get up from the barstool and wander across the floor and under the balcony of the bar toward the stage. I hoist myself up onto the stairs then roll under the curtain and lie on my back. I briefly stare up at the domed ceiling before I push to my feet and take a seat on the bench in front of the piano. My fingers lightly graze the keys, the off-key noise echoing in the emptiness around me.

It's not that I'm alone a lot. I have Lila and Ethan at home. My brother Dean and his wife Caroline visit occasionally, and they bring my niece Scarlett, who has so much energy it's impossible to have enough downtime to focus anything. Plus, when I get really restless, I sometimes fly up to Star Grove and visit my father and his girlfriend.

I do feel lonely, though, a lot more than I like to admit. It's not like I'd ever leave Micha over having to live alone. I knew what I was getting into when I married him. It would just be nice if the tours would ease up just a tiny bit so we could actually spend more than a few weeks together every few months.

"Ella, what are you doing up here?" Micha suddenly says from behind me.

I spin around on the bench, startled so badly my heart slams against my chest. "Jesus, you scared me," I say breathlessly. Then I lower my hand and savor the sight of him.

Dressed head to toe in black, he nearly blends in with the inadequate lighting of the stage. My fingers twitch to feel the muscles of his lean body and his soft, sandy blonde hair that hangs in his aqua eyes. My lips are desperate to taste his lip ring. God, I fucking love that lip ring.

He softly chuckles. "You know, I could take a picture if you want. It'll last longer."

I smile up at him. "I just might ask you to do that."

He moves around the bench and plops down beside me. His fingers align with the keys, and the notes he creates sound a lot more like music than the noise I was just making.

"You looked sad," he tells me as he rests his fingers on his legs.

I shake my head as I turn around on the bench and face the piano again. "No, I was just bored and passing time."

"Are you sure?" His fingers enfold around my knee. "You know you can talk to me about anything, including if you're sad or if some blonde crazy girl said something to you that was completely inappropriate."

"How did you find out about that?"

"Jerry, the bouncer, told me about her." He sighs. "I'm so sorry she said that stuff to you. You know it's not true, right?"

"Of course I know it's not true. Micha, trust me, if I've learned anything about our relationship over the last six years, it's that I can trust you and tell you anything. And I didn't tell you about crazy Blondie because it doesn't matter. You love me—that's what matters." I bring my leg up and rest my chin on my knee. "Now, enough talk about me. It's your turn for *you* to tell *me* what's wrong. Because I know there's something bothering you."

He stares at his fingers massaging my kneecap. "I hate burdening you with my problems."

I cup his scruffy cheek and force him to look at me. "It's never a burden. I promise."

He swallows hard. "I think I'm just tired."

"Of this?" I point at the stage.

"Maybe, not necessarily the singing part, but the touring part, Mike, the label ... They're all getting on my nerves." He turns around in the seat and stretches his legs out as he reclines back against the piano. "They're trying to change my image. They want me to turn into the cliché, tortured, slutty, rock singer."

"I'm so sorry." I lace my fingers through his. "You know I'm here for you, whatever you do or whoever you choose to be."

He brushes his hair out of his aqua eyes. "I know you are." He smoothes the pad of his thumb across my black-stoned wedding ring. "I just worry that, if I make the wrong choice, I'll ruin our future."

"Our future's going to be fine." I give his hand a squeeze, fighting back the tears. More tours? A sluttier image? Yeah, there goes any hope for incidents like with the blonde hair puller to stop. "Even if you have to be a slutty manwhore."

He snorts a laugh as he traces the folds in his fingers. "Yeah, well, I'm glad you think so." He flips my hand over and sketches the lines of my palm. "Okay, enough sad talk. Tell me something new."

I rack my brain for a response. "Um, well, Lila and Ethan bought a new car."

He stares blankly at me. "That's all you got? Come on, pretty girl, I want some happy news."

I shrug. "Sorry. Nothing's really happened. Us common folks live pretty boring lives." I search for something else to tell him, something better. "Oh, yeah." I smack my free hand against my forehead. "Dean and Caroline are having another baby."

"Really?" He doesn't seem as happy as I've thought he would, his lips twitching to turn downward. "When?"

"I think she's just over three months pregnant, so she'll have the baby in April." I study his expression carefully, wondering what's troubling him now.

He bobs his head up and down, nodding distractedly as he develops a sudden interest in his boots. "That's nice. I'll have to make sure to call and congratulate them."

22

"Make sure to sound more happy when you do, though." I'm not sure what to say to him. Either he's still sulky over his job or about the fact that he'll soon have another niece or nephew and still no daughter or son. I wish I could fix both for him; but, the first problem is out of my hands and the second I'm just not ready to deal with yet. Yes, I love him more than anything, but my fear of being a mother is still astronomical.

A slow breath eases from his lips as his gaze collides with mine. "Sorry. I'm being a downer, aren't I?" He leans toward me, tucking a strand of hair behind my ear. "That isn't fair to you after you flew across the country to see me."

"Micha, you should know by now"—I press my lips together, trying not to laugh as I prepare to quote a line from one of his songs—"that *I would travel to hell and back just to be with you.*"

"Ha, ha," he says playfully, sticking out his tongue. "You wound my heart, Ella May. I wrote those lyrics for you and you mock me with them."

"I'm not mocking, just having fun—"

He cuts me off as he nips at my bottom lip, eliciting a soul-bearing groan from me. He slowly starts unbuttoning my shirt, picking up the pace the farther down he gets until he finally becomes so impatient he rips the fabric off.

"I miss your kisses the most." I willingly lean against the piano as he unfastens my bra and urges me back.

He quickly stands up to tug his shirt over his head and then places an arm on each side of me as his body hovers over mine. "I miss everything the most," he says before he kisses me. "All the fucking time. I swear to God, I need to see you more."

My legs fasten around his waist as the ivory keys dig into my flesh. My fingers trace the outlines of his muscular stomach, the inscription of his tattoos, feeling his heart slamming erratically against his chest.

Excitement bursts to the surface when he pushes back to undo the button on my jeans.

"Micha, wait." I pant. "Are we really going to do this?"

"Do what?" He teases me with a cock of his brow as he gradually unzips my jeans.

I kick off my shoes while I gasp for air. "Have sex on a piano."

He pulls my jeans and panties off, his passionate gaze skimming every inch of my flesh, stifling my eager body with overpowering heat.

"You sound so excited about the idea," he says as I

24

reach for the top of his pants and unflick the button.

"I'll take it wherever I can get it." I sit up and yank his jeans down. "Besides, we can add it to our growing list of strange places we've had sex. I think this one might earn the number three spot, right below backstage at a concert, wrapped in the curtain."

Instead of smiling, his happiness falters. "I promise I'm going to find a way to change all this, pretty girl. You deserve so much better than this."

Before I can respond, his lips come down hard on mine, scorching hot as he spreads my legs open and slips two fingers deep inside me.

"Micha... I..." My head falls back and my body arches into his touch, fervently seeking more of him.

"You feel so good," he whispers against my mouth. "God dammit, Ella. I miss this way too much."

"Me... too..." I trail off. I can barely think straight, let alone form coherent words.

His lips suddenly leave mine, and he leans back to watch as his fingers drive me toward the edge. His free hand finds my nipple and softly pinches, causing sheer bliss to coil and rush through my body. A helpless moan escapes my lips, and his aqua eyes darken to an ocean blue.

"You're so fucking gorgeous, Ella. I swear to God, I

just want to write songs about how you look right now."

I want to tell him no way, that I don't want to have the entire world knowing what I look like when I'm about to orgasm, yet I'm too far gone to care. "You can write whatever you want as long as you keep touching me like this."

His eyes blaze with lust while he continues to feel me from the inside and the out. His mouth lowers to mine again, his tongue urging my lips apart. The scent of him is intoxicating, adding intensity to the moment as my thoughts drift to all the times we've spent exactly like this.

I just wish there were more.

So many more.

All my worries swiftly evaporate, though, as something deep inside me shatters. I cry out as I struggle to grasp onto the feeling. Fire. Intensity. Warmth. Heat. I feel it all.

Micha's mouth is abruptly leaving mine along with his body, and instantly, my body is submersed in coldness. I'm about to beg him to come back to me, but then he grips my thighs and raises my hips as he leans back over me.

With one swift rock, he thrusts deep. The sensation is so intense I forget to breathe and have to fight to remain conscious. My muscles are wound tight, eager to let go. Every part of me pleads to be filled completely as his hips grind against mine, and my back bangs against the piano. The keys noisily chime over our panting, and the sound echoes around us. I'd be worried someone will hear it and come onto the stage to see what's happening, but I'm way too lost in the feel of Micha on me, inside me, engulfing me.

My fingers pierce his shoulder blades, desperate to clutch on for just a little bit longer, desperate to have just a bit more time with him. But, within a few short minutes, I come way too soon, crying out over the sound of the piano.

Micha soon joins me, kissing me all the way to the end while he gives a final rock inside me. I arch my back at the last second so he can sink even deeper inside, moaning at the pulsating sensation. Micha must love the feeling, too, because he lets out the loudest, slowest, most savoring groan I've ever heard leave his lips.

"That was…" He gasps for oxygen as he stares intently into my eyes.

"Fucking awesome," I finish for him, pressing my sweaty chest to his, not ready for him to leave me just yet.

The corners of his lips quirk. "Stole the words right out of my mouth, pretty girl."

I smile, tired yet content. "I just wish I didn't have to fly out tonight."

His expression plummets, and he jerks back. "I thought you were staying with me for the weekend?"

"I was, but then the gallery decided to have a last minute show, and I don't want Gena there by herself, trying to handle everything." I reach up and try to brush away the lines between his brows, but my touch only deepens the sadness etching his face. "I thought I mentioned it on the phone the other day."

"You might have." He backs away from me and collects his boxers from the floor. "I've been really distracted lately and might not have heard you or something."

He slips his boxers and jeans back on while I pick up my pants and shirt from the floor. We finish getting dressed in silence, the elation I felt when I landed earlier slipping farther and farther away.

"I'm going to fix this," he mumbles as I'm buttoning my shirt.

"Fix what?" When I glance up at him, the fierceness in his eyes causes me to shrink back.

"This distance between us." He yanks his shirt over his head and gestures between us. "Things are going to change. I promise." He pauses, and then his lips curve to a smile. "In fact, I want to make a pact. Right here. Right now."

"Aren't we a little too old for pacts?" I ask as I wiggle

my foot into my boot.

He shakes his head. "We'll never be too old for pacts. *Ever.*"

A faint smile graces my lips as I tie my boot. "So what's the pact going to be this time, my dear husband?" I ask as I stand back upright.

His eyes raise to the ceiling as he considers something, then his gaze falls back on me. He raises his hand to his mouth and spits into his palm. "In two months, I won't be on the road anymore. I'll be working my job in San Diego only and be living with you all the damn time, like I dream about every night. Infinitely and always."

"Two months? That seems like a really short time to make that plan happen."

"Yeah, but I can't stand it any longer. Two months is my time limit before I go crazy." He extends his hand to me, waiting for me to spit and shake on it.

Even though I'm skeptical, I spit into my palm and thread my fingers through his. "Okay, Micha Scott, you have a deal."

His eyes light up like they used to every Fourth of July when his mom would set off fireworks. "See you in two months?"

I nod, my grip on his hand tightening. "See you in two

months." I lean in and press my lips to his, sealing the deal with a kiss.

Chapter 3

Two Months Later…

Ella

My bed in my San Diego home feels cold and empty. It's felt this way for a while but has gotten worse over the last two months while Micha's been on the road, finishing up his tour. It's as if my body suddenly craves more of him, like it finally realizes just how starved it's been for Micha's touch and warmth.

For the first few years, I used to travel with him. Some of my best moments happened during those trips, and I created some of my best art. But, after opening up my own gallery, I had to sit the last few tours out to keep on top of business. And, quite honestly, I like my life. But I can't wait until tonight when the bed will be warm again. Because, Micha plays his final tour performance in San Diego tonight, and then he's home to keep the bed warm with me again.

I'm not sure how long he'll be here this time. He hasn't mentioned anything yet about whether or not he will be able to pull the pact off. I highly doubt it. When he made the vow to both of us back on the stage, I knew his words were based on his emotions and not reality. The reality is that he's a singer. That he loves making music. Loves what he does, despite missing me. What's more, in order to keep doing what he loves, he has to make his label and producer happy, which means conforming when he needs to. I only hope one day down the road things can change for him.

I sigh as I think of the many years ahead of me where the bed will remain cold and empty. Where crazy fans will pull my hair and threaten me. Where I miss him so much it hurts.

My thoughts start sinking to a dark place, but I instantly force them out of my head. No, I'm not going to fixate on depressing stuff today. Just one more day is all I have to make it through before I get to wake up with Micha, one of my favorite things about being married. Well, that and the kissing. Secret sharing. Unconditional love.

Okay, maybe there are a lot of things I love about being married.

That and Micha has kind of turned me into a sap over the last five years.

My plans for the day are to sleep in as late as possible to pass the time until I have to head down to The Bronze Key to watch Micha play. But, as the sun rises over the city, my phone begins vibrating from my nightstand, forcing me to wake up.

I sit up in the bed and reach for my phone. "Hello?" I answer, rubbing the sleepiness from my eyes.

"What are you doing?" My friend, Lila Summers, practically shouts from the other end. I know her well enough to understand that the urgency in her tone could be exaggerated.

"Not much." I glance at the antique clock on the wall as I stretch my hands above my head. Dammit. *It's only a little after nine in the morning. I wanted to sleep in so much later.* "But what are you doing calling me so early?"

"Because I have an emergency."

My body goes as rigid as a board while worry seeps into my bones. "Is everything okay? You sound like you're flipping out."

"That's because I am." She lets out a disgruntled sigh. "Ethan's been acting weird lately."

Shaking my head, I instantly relax. "Lila, he always acts weird."

"Ella," she huffs, "this is important. He's acting like… well, like he's going to break up with me."

"I highly doubt that."

"How? How can you not doubt it when I can."

"Um, because he's totally in love with you." I swing

my feet out of bed and plant them firmly onto the hard-wood floor. "Has been for years."

"Yeah, but…" She trails off. I know where her mind is heading. The fact that they aren't married after five years of being together bothers the crap out of Lila. "I just wish we were husband and wife. It would make the fear of him leaving me a lot less intense."

"Husbands leave wives all the time. Having a ring on your finger doesn't make feelings change. If he was going to leave you, he would, regardless. It's the same way with anyone, really." I rise to my feet and pad over to the curtains, throwing them open.

The floor to ceiling windows allow an abundance of sunshine inside my bedroom and give me the most awesome view of the city. I remember when Micha and I bought the two-story home after his songs really started selling. It was the view that won me over. For Micha, it was the large, "sex-worthy" bathtub in the master bathroom.

"Jeez, Ella, you never sugarcoat anything," Lila says with a heavy sigh.

"Sorry. My head just went to a really weird place." I push open the double doors and walk out onto the balcony.

The winter air kisses my damp skin as I rest my arms

on the railing and gaze at the clear blue sky. I'm not sure why, but I've been overheating lately, especially in the mornings. While most people are in jackets, I usually sport shorts and get a lot of strange looks because of it. It's actually starting to concern me a little that maybe something might be wrong.

"A mom place?" Lila asks concernedly, interrupting my overheating concerns.

"No, not really. It's strange, but mom thoughts have been pretty mellow for the last year or so, even around the holidays and summer."

"That's good. It probably means you're healed."

"Well, I wouldn't go that far. It just means I've come to terms with what is."

"You sound so wise," she remarks. "Seriously, Ella, I'm so proud of you. I wish I could let all my family shit go."

"You can," I tell her as I shut my eyes and breathe in the fresh air. "All you have to do is accept what is and let go."

"You mean stop talking to my parents? Because I kind of have."

I open my eyes. "I know, but you haven't fully let go."

"I'm working on it. It's just hard with the inheritance.

It was my mother's mom who left it to me, and therefore, she thinks she's entitled to occasionally call me up and see what I'm doing."

"You could always stop answering the phone." I turn around and lean against the railing.

"Yeah, I probably should." She releases a stressed breath. "Okay, no more family talk. I called to chat about Ethan, not my crazy bitch of a mother. I just wish he'd change his mind about marriage, like you did."

"Hey, I never was completely against marriage," I argue. "Just getting that fully committed to someone."

"His isn't because of a commitment thing; he just doesn't want to turn into his parents."

"Which I can kind of understand, seeing as how I worried for years that I'd end up like my mother." I pause, glancing at the next door neighbor's two-story home. "Can I be really honest with you?"

"You know I prefer it that way."

"Even if it stings?"

"Of course. If I didn't want the truth, I would have never called you."

I sink into a chair and spit it out. "The thing is, with as long as Ethan has dragged out this non-marriage idea, I'm kind of starting to believe that his mind may never change.

Maybe he will remain unmarried for his entire life." I bite down on my lip as I wait for her response. She's silent for an eternity, and I worry I've said the wrong thing.

"I know," she finally utters. "I think I've known that for a few years. I'm just too terrified to accept it."

"And that's understandable." I rise to my feet when I hear the neighbor's sliding glass door open. Moments later, Lila strolls out of the two-story house similar to mine and onto the deck that stretches out across the backyard. Our homes are so close, if we both extended our arms, we could hold hands.

Ethan and Lila moved in less than a year ago after Lila received her inheritance. Lila is content with staying at home most of the time, but Ethan had to find a job; otherwise, "he'd go mad crazy." He ended up opening his own tour guide place with Lila's help, and the two of them seem really happy except for the marriage thing.

"You know, you could have just come over," I call out to her, hanging up the phone.

"I wasn't sure if you were awake." She pulls her long, blonde hair up into a messy bun then pads over to the edge of the balcony. She ties the sash of her satin robe, and rests her arms against the wooden railing. "Tell me what to do, Ella. I need to know what to do."

I frown. "I'm probably one of the worst people to give advice."

She swiftly shakes her head. "No, you're not. You only think you are."

"Yes, I am." I offer an apologetic look when her mood plunges. "Sorry, but even if I was the most spectacular person in the world to give advice, it's really about what you want. Either you can accept that you might just be Ethan's girlfriend for forever and come to terms with that or you can't and move on."

Her shoulders sag. "I want to be okay with it. I mean, we're basically like husband and wife. We're even trying to have kids and everything."

My lips part in shock. "Since when?!"

She shrugs. "For, like, the last year."

I span my hands out to the side. "Why didn't you tell me this?"

She snorts a laugh. "You, the queen of 'I Never Want to Be a Mother.' Yeah, I learned a long time ago that kid talk and you just don't mix."

I point a finger at her. "Hey, I'm not that bad anymore."

She undecidedly wavers. "All right, I'll give you that. But you still get really squimish over anything kid related."

"True, but I did hold your sister's baby the other day without getting too wigged out. And I talk with Caroline about her pregnancy on the phone all the time. In fact, I helped her plan how to surprise Dean with the news. I don't really get why there's a need to surprise a husband with the news that he's procreated, but hey, whatever floats her boat."

She stares me down. "Okay, yes, I'll give it to you that you've kind of evolved. But I bet you're getting uncomfortable just talking about it right now."

I shake my head. "Nope."

Her eyes sparkle mischievously. "Okay, Mrs. Calm, how about if I ask you when you and Micha are going to have your own kids."

I suddenly grow extremely uncomfortable. I usually am when it comes to thinking about having kids of my own. "Fine, you win that one. But, seriously, that was a low blow."

"What can I say? I know how to kick you where it counts." She smiles, but it's forced.

I glance back at my house, racking my brain for a way to cheer her up because it's my friend duty to do so. As my gaze lands on my closet, an idea sparkles.

"I have an idea that will maybe clear your head." I

look back at her and grin.

She perks up, her posture straightening. "And what's your idea? Please tell me it's something epically fun because I need epically fun."

"Well, I need a new outfit for the concert tonight if you're interested in helping me find one."

"Wow. You must really feel sorry for me if you're suggesting we go shopping." A grin lights up her face and it almost makes the next four hours of store time less painful to endure. "Meet me down at the car in like thirty?"

I nod as I back toward the door. "But we have to stop for coffee."

She opens the back door to her house. "Of course. An Ella with no caffeine is never fun."

Smiling, I retreat inside my bedroom and shut the door behind me. The inside of my house is almost as equally beautiful as the view of the city. Filled with antique furniture and art, the walls and rooms have character. The hardwood floors look purposefully old, and the walls are painted in various different colors that breathe life into the place. My favorite room is the attic, though, because it's where I create my art.

After I take a quick shower, I pull on a pair of denim shorts and a black shirt then apply some kohl liner around my eyes. Right on cue, a spout of nausea slams against my stomach as I'm brushing my long, auburn hair.

"Shit." I drop to my knees in front of the toilet. Since I haven't had breakfast yet, I end up dry heaving for about a minute before my stomach settles, and I stumble to my feet again.

Dammit. This shit is getting really old. Between the overheating and the vomiting, I think it might be time to go to the doctor to make sure something's not wrong.

I reapply my makeup then change into a fresh shirt before heading out of the house. The sun is gleaming in the sky, the air smells like cut grass, and my neighbor, Mrs. Flicking, waves to me as I round the fence to Lila's driveway.

The garage door is open, and Lila is waiting for me by her shiny black Mercedes. She's changed into a flowery sundress and a jacket, her long, blonde hair is down and wavy, and she's texting someone as I approach her.

"Jesus, you look like shit," she remarks when she glances up at me.

"Wow. Thanks. Exactly what every woman wants to hear right before they go shopping for something to make them look sexy for their husband, who they haven't seen in two months." I sling my purse over my shoulder as I open

41

the passenger door of the car.

"I'm so sorry." She ducks into the car and starts up the engine. "I didn't mean to sound like such a bitch." She squints at me. "But you do look really pale."

"I got sick this morning," I admit as I fan my hand in front of my face. "And can we please keep the heat off this time? I feel like I'm burning up all the damn time. I'm seriously wondering if I've had the longest flu ever or something."

With a pucker at her brows, she reaches across the console and places the palm of her hand on my forehead. "You don't feel like you have a fever." She lowers her hand to the shifter and pushes it into reverse. "Are you sure you're up for shopping today? Because, if you're not feeling good, we can just sit home and watch a movie or something. That cheers me up, too, just as long as I can pick the movie."

I motion for her to back up the car. "No way. We're so doing this. I need a dress, and you need cheering up."

"Thank you, best friend." She beams as she backs down the driveway.

"No problem." I draw the seatbelt over my shoulder. "I just wish I knew what was up with me."

She adjusts her mirror as she nears the street. "Up with

what?"

"These stupid nausea spouts I've been having for like a month."

She abruptly slams on the brakes, sending the car lurching to a stop. I shoot forward in my seat, nearly banging my head on the dash.

"What the hell, Lila?" I brush stray strands of hair out of my eyes and turn my head to gape at her. "What was that about?"

Her blue eyes search mine. "You said you've been getting sick to your stomach for like a month?"

I nod, confused. "Yeah. So? It's probably stress or the flu. But don't worry, if it keeps up, I'll go to the doctor."

She scans my outfit over. "And you're wearing shorts when it's nearly Christmas."

"Okay, that is a little bit weird," I agree with her. "But I'm so freaking hot all the time I can't stand wearing anything warmer."

A slow grin expands across her face. "Oh, my God, El-la!" She claps her hands and squeals, "You're pregnant!"

I deflate like a balloon. "Are you fucking crazy! No, I'm not!"

She flinches from the sharpness in my tone but continues to smile. "Ella, I know you and Micha haven't really decided to try having kids yet, but trust me, you show signs of being pregnant. I search the internet all the time for this stuff."

"So what?" I squeak, sounding very unlike me. "Just because the internet says something doesn't mean it's true."

"Okay." She pauses then decides to tread forward despite my horror over the subject. "When was your last period?"

I stare at the ceiling as I mentally calculate. When I finally realize it was a little over two months ago, right before Micha and I had hot, sweaty piano bench sex, fear soars through me so potently I can barely breathe. How is this freaking possible? I mean, I'm on the damn pill. There was that week that I missed a few and had to start over, though. Fuck, I forgot about that.

I bite at my fingernails. *Shit.*

"Things have been so intense at the gallery I can barely remember to eat, let alone when the last time I had my period was," I lie, unable to accept the truth.

Lila pats my hand. "Oh, Ella."

I jerk away from her. "Don't you 'oh Ella' me."

She surrenders, her hands in front of her. "Okay, Miss Hormones."

"Lila!" I whine as tears sting my eyes. "Stop with the

jokes. I'm freaking out here."

Her hands fall to her lap. "Sorry. What do you need from me?"

"For you to help me. *Please*," I practically beg her, but for what, I'm not even sure. Something that will help me handle this.

She must understand me because she nods and then backs out onto the road. "Okay, help is on the way."

"Where are we going?" I ask, telling myself to breathe. That it can't be true. That it's a mistake. That it has to be a mistake. Because I was never supposed to be a mother.

She steers the car toward the city. "To find out the truth."

Life has thrown me a curveball that's hit me straight in the face. My brain aches so badly I can hardly think straight, much less process my emotions. I honestly wish I couldn't think at all, then maybe I wouldn't have to acknowledge the reality in front of me.

"How accurate are these things?" I ask Lila as I stare at the five pregnancy tests scattered on my bathroom counter-top. All show positive, that yes, there's a human growing in my stomach. Each time I think about it, I want to throw up. *Mom? I'm not a mom.*

"Pretty accurate," Lila says as she reads the back of the box. Once she's finished, she hops off the counter and tosses the box into the trashcan. "Face it, Ella, I think you have a bun in your oven."

"Ew. Don't ever say that." I frown at the stupid tests again. "Are you sure there's not a small chance that all of them could be wrong?"

She shrugs as she checks her reflection in the mirror, wiping a dab of lipstick from her teeth. "There might be, but with five positives, I doubt it."

I squeeze my eyes shut, feeling the floor crumbling beneath me. "Now what do I do?" I whisper.

When she places her hands on my shoulders, my eyelids open. "You tell Micha." She looks over my shoulder and at me in the mirror. "And then you two get to celebrate."

Lila is obviously happy about this and thinks I should be equally as happy. She doesn't know—doesn't understand—my fear of being a mother. From the day Micha and I first started talking about having children, I worried I couldn't be a mother. That, if I had a child of my own, I wouldn't know what to do with it since my own mother never seemed to know what to do with me. I actually spent many years taking care of her until I was about seventeen, and she took her own life. Left this world.

And now I'm supposed to bring someone into this world?

"I think I need to get ready for the concert," I mumble, offering Lila a fake smile when she narrows her eyes at me.

"Let me know how it goes," she replies as she turns to leave. Then she pauses in the doorway and looks over her shoulder at me. "And, Ella, be happy. This is a happy thing, okay?"

My smile grows even faker. "Okay."

Her smile seems as sad as mine, but at the moment, I don't have the energy to pick us both up.

Once she leaves the bathroom, I slam the door shut and collapse to my knees on the tile floor. God, I wish I had someone a little more understanding to talk to, wish I had a mother to call up and ask for advice. But, all I have is a father who hardly ever was a father to me until I was about twenty.

Lila, even though she means well, is too excited over this. She doesn't get the undiluted terror I feel just thinking those test could be true. The sheer and utter horror over the fact that I might be a mother soon, and I have absolutely no idea what that entails.

As the realization weighs on me, I lie down on the

floor, and for the first time in a long time, I cry my heart out.

Chapter 4

Micha

Ella doesn't show up at my final performance for the tour, and her phone is sending me straight to voicemail every time I call her. I'm trying not to lose my shit over not being able to get a hold of her. More than likely, she's locked herself up in the attic to paint and has lost track of time—it's happened before.

I had such huge plans for us tonight. Dinner after the concert, dancing, sex, going home, sex, talking about what's going on in my career. Sex. Sex. Sex. But, as I pull up to our house and see that all the lights are off, my worry rockets through the roof.

I quickly park the car in the garage, silence the engine, and then rush into the house. The alarm doesn't go off, which means it wasn't set, making my worry escalate.

"Ella!" I call out as I drop the car keys onto the kitchen counter and dash for the stairway. "Ella, baby, are you home?"

When I reach the top of the stairs, I hurry to our bedroom door and push it open. Immediately, my heart settles.

Ella is curled up in a ball on the bed, fast asleep.

I cross the room, sink down on the edge of the mattress beside her, and watch her sleep peacefully, softly breathing in and out.

"God, I'm so glad to be home," I whisper as I kick my boots off.

As they thud against the floor, Ella's eyelids flutter open. She glances up at me, bleary eyed and disoriented. "Am I dreaming?" she asks as her gaze skims the room then lands back on me.

I sweep her hair out of her eyes. "No, baby, this isn't a dream. I'm here."

"What about earlier today?" she mutters as she sits up in bed and stretches her arms above her head. "Was that a dream?"

My brows furrow. "What happened earlier today?"

Her gaze flicks to the bathroom door, then she blinks back to me. "Nothing. I just got sick." She yawns then slumps against the headboard. "I feel so tired."

"I'm sorry you're sick." I slip off my other boot then climb over her and lay down in the bed. "It feels so good to be in my own bed again." I bury my head into the pillow and stretch out my arms.

She nods then suddenly her eyes widen. "Oh, my word, I missed your performance, didn't I?" Her gaze darts to the midnight sky outside the window and the city lights that look like a thousand fireflies dusting the land. "I'm so sorry, Micha." Shaking her head, she lies down in the bed beside me so we're lying on the mattress, facing each other. "I can't believe I missed it. One minute, I was getting ready, and the next, I got sick, and then..." She shudders. "Well, I guess I laid down and fell asleep."

"It's okay," I assure her with an exhausted grin. "There are a thousand ways you can make it up to me."

She smiles tiredly. "Oh, yeah?"

"Definitely," I murmur, my gaze dropping to her lips.

I imagine I lean forward to kiss her, but the next thing I know, I'm opening my eyes to warm sunlight filtering through the bedroom.

"Rise and shine, beautiful boy," Ella singsongs as she leans over me with the world's most heart-stopping smile on her face.

"What happened? I swear I was talking to you like five seconds ago, and it was nighttime." I blink up at her then leisurely take in her perky nipples through the fabric of her tank top. Unable to help myself, I reach up and graze one with my thumb.

"We both fell asleep. Guess we're getting super old." She shivers, wiggling out of my touch. When I frown, she forces a smile as she reaches for my mouth and fiddles with my lip ring, tracing her fingertip over the metal.

"Or just super overworked." My fingers find her waist, and my nails delve into her flesh. "We should just relax all day. And I know the perfect way to do that." I eagerly move up to kiss her lips.

She covers my mouth with her hand, stopping me for the second time in thirty seconds.

What the hell?

"As much as I'd love to get the relaxing day started," she says as she withdraws her hand, "I have to go to the doctor first."

I pout. "Well, that's no fun."

"Neither is having sex with a sick person."

"Wouldn't be the first time."

She shakes her head as she scoots to the edge of the bed and lowers her feet to the floor. "I know, but my appointment is in like thirty minutes, and it takes fifteen just to get to the doctor's office." Her voice quivers toward the end.

My brow crooks as I sit up. "Something's wrong. I can tell."

"No, everything's fine," she insists as she bolts from the bed and toward the bathroom. "I just need to get my ass cleaned up and on the road. That's all. Otherwise, I'll miss my appointment." With that, she shuts the door, leaving me utterly confused.

My confusion only increases when she leaves the house so quickly she barely kisses me good-bye. But, the real kicker is when I wander out to the garage and see that her GTO is still parked beside my Chevelle.

"So what the hell did she drive to the doctor's office with?" Scratching my head, I push on the garage opener. Once the door is fully open, I hike down the driveway toward Ethan and Lila's house.

The neighborhood is completely different from where Ella and I grew up. Instead of drug dealers on the street corners and old cars decorating the yards, there are Christmas decorations everywhere and green grass. The entire neighborhood is decked out with holiday decorations: Christmas trees, tinsel, lights, snowman created from artificial snow. The only two on the block that don't declare the holiday cheer are Ethan's and mine. Usually, it's not that big of a deal—I'm never home for too long around the holidays to let it bother me—but this year is different.

I need to change some stuff.

Start some traditions.

I give a quick glimpse into their garage and note that

Ethan's truck is inside, but Lila's car is missing. Maybe Lila drove her. The question is, why?

Deciding I need to get to the bottom of what's going on, I go straight to the source. I bang on the front door of Ethan and Lila's house as hard as I can. Ethan has turned into the heaviest sleeper over the last couple of years, and knowing this, I continue to ring the doorbell over and over again until he finally throws open the front door.

He has bags under his eyes, his brown hair is disheveled, and he looks cranky as shit. "What the fuck, man?" Ethan says as he tugs a T-shirt over his head.

"What? No welcome home hug?" I joke. While he blinks, unimpressed, I squeeze by him and let myself into his home.

"Come in," he mutters grumpily as he closes the door behind me.

I grin at him, noting the air smells like cookies. "Did Lila bake this morning?"

"Chocolate chip, I think," he says as he heads across the living room. "You are way too cheery for me this morning."

"Don't pretend you didn't miss my cheeriness."

He rolls his eyes yet doesn't deny it.

I follow him inside the kitchen and snatch three cookies off a plate that's on the table. As much as I love Ella, Lila has turned into a fantastic cook, and just the smell of the cookies causes my mouth to salivate.

"Do you know how lucky you are to get to eat this stuff every day?" I say as I stuff my mouth full of chocolate gooiness. "I usually get fast food for breakfast."

"Of course I know how lucky I am," he snaps, snatching up a cookie himself. "I think about it all the damn time."

I raise my hands up. "Whoa. Sorry, man. I didn't mean to push a button."

He blows out a breath as he slumps down on a stool by the counter. "No, I'm sorry. I didn't mean to go all mad crazy on you." He lowers his head into his hands. "I'm just stressed out about shit."

I take another bite of the cookie. "Is this about the marriage thing?"

His head whips up, his face draining of color. "How did you know about that?"

"Ella told me."

"But how did she know about it?"

I break off a corner of one of the cookies and pop it into my mouth. "Um, because you guys are always fighting about it."

"Wait? What marriage thing are you talking about?"

"Well, I was talking about how you two are always arguing over marriage." I lick off a glob of melted chocolate from my hand. "But now I'm starting to wonder if it's something else."

If it's possible, he looks even paler. "Can I show you something?" he asks intensely.

I briefly hesitate. "Depends on what that something is. Because you have this weird look on your face that's kind of creeping me out."

"Come on, man. I'm being serious." He pushes back from the counter and stands up from the seat. "I need to show somebody something; otherwise, I'm going to fucking lose my goddamn mind."

"Oh, fine." I scarf down the rest of the cookie. "I'll let you pile your secret on me, just as long as you tell me why Lila took Ella to the doctor this morning."

He shrugs as we walk out of the kitchen. "Beats the shit out of me." He pauses in front of the stairway. "Wait. I think Lila said something about going to town and doing something."

I grip at the railing. "Like what?"

"That, I can't help you with." He starts up the stairs.

"Well, that doesn't help much," I say as I trudge after

him.

"Sorry, but it's all I got." He turns right when we reach the top of the stairway and heads down the hallway toward his bedroom. "The two of them are literally driving me crazy, man. I mean, I love Lila, and Ella is okay sometimes, but"—he glances over his shoulder at me as he pushes open the bedroom door—"I spend all my time with the two of them, and I'm starting to go nuts with all their girlie crap."

"Don't you have any other guys to hang out with?" I ask as he enters his bedroom.

He rolls his eyes. "Yeah, because my sparkling personality gets me so many friends."

I laugh while I wander in after him, glancing around his room at the photos of Lila and him on the wall. The two of them have gotten to spend so much time together that it makes me feel jealous. No more, though. No more missing birthdays, anniversaries, or holidays.

"Well, I might be around a little bit more."

His brows elevate as he opens the top dresser drawer. "Really? You get Mike to ease up on the touring or something?"

I shake my head. "I can't really say anything for sure yet. I have to talk to Ella about stuff first."

"Well, I hope it works out that you aren't gone all the

time," he says as he reaches into the drawer. "For her sake and mine."

I open my mouth to retort a funny comeback about him being needy, but once I catch sight of what he has in his hand, my humor vanishes. "You really have lost your damn mind, haven't you?"

He looks absolutely horrified as he nods. "I think I'm in deep shit."

Chapter 5

Ella

Christmas tunes play from the car stereo, promising happy days of holiday joy ahead. I wonder if I'll ever feel happy again after what was just revealed to me in one of the stale smelling rooms at the doctor's office.

"Oh, my God, I hope it's a girl," Lila says excitedly as we drive down the freeway toward our subdivision. "Then we get to dress her up in cute, little dresses."

I scrunch my nose. "No dresses." I picture a little, baby girl with blonde hair and green eyes, punked out in black pants, boots, and maybe a shirt with a skeleton. Then I shake my head. *What the hell am I doing?*

"Stop talking about the sex. I'm still trying to process what just happened."

She bites down on her lip as she veers into the next lane and then down the exit ramp. "But you have to admit it, shopping for a girl would be so cool," she sputters out, unable to contain her enthusiasm for more than five seconds. "We should totally stop by a store right now."

"No way." I chew on my thumbnail, trying not to panic, but suppressing my anxiety is becoming more complicated by the second.

The doctor confirmed the tests. I'm pregnant. My body is now home to a mini me. *Oh, my God, I think I'm going to puke again.*

I clutch at my stomach. "I just want to get home."

"Oh, fine, you party pooper." She sulks. "But I will shop for it sooner or later, even if it's a boy." She releases a deafening exhale then mutters, "It'll probably be my only chance, anyway."

"Fuck." I suddenly feel like such a jerk. "I'm so sorry, Lila. I didn't even think about how you were trying and then"—I motion my hand in the direction of my stomach—"this happens."

"Ella, let's get one thing straight," she says, gripping the wheel. "I'm super happy for you, regardless of what's going on with me."

"But you're sad," I note as I slip my sunglasses on to block out the sunlight reflecting through the window. "I can see it in your eyes that you are."

She sucks in a slow inhale as her gaze remains glued to the road. "I just worry that it's not ever going to happen for me."

"Having a baby?"

"That, and that I'll end up a middle-aged, single woman living with my cat named Chester that I talk to out loud."

"Lila, Ethan's not ever going to leave you."

She stares at her ring finger. "Maybe. But maybe not."

"Hey." I reach over and cover her hand, preparing to tell her how wrong she is, but I've told her it enough that I don't think she'll ever believe it. So, I decide to go a different direction. "I'll tell you what. If Ethan decides to leave you, you can move in with Micha and I so you won't be all alone."

Her lips threaten to turn upward. "Really? Can I even have the guest bedroom near the attic? Because that's my favorite room in the house."

I nod. "And your future cat Chester can come, too, if you want."

Laughter erupts from her lips. "Fine, you have a deal, but only if I get to help take care of little Ella."

I frown as I slump back in the seat. For a moment, I almost forgot about being pregnant. "Sounds like a deal to me. You'll probably be a better mother, anyway."

She gives me a stern look that I shy away from. Without scolding me, though, she flips on the blinker to make a turn down our street. We zoom past the houses glammed up in Christmas décor, lights, Santa's, and giant snow globes.

Christmas is in a week, and Micha and my house remains holiday-less. It's not because I'm a Grinch; I've just never been into Christmas. It suddenly feels like I should be, though.

"When are you going to tell Micha?" Lila abruptly asks. "I mean, it's great that I got to come to your appointment today, but he really should be a part of it. And, knowing him, he's going to want to."

"I know he will." Shutting my eyes, I rest my head against the window and bask in the sunlight. "I'll tell him. I just have to talk to someone first."

"Who? Your dad or something? Because it seems a little strange to tell him before Micha."

I open my eyes and look over at her. "No, not him. That would be way weird." Honestly, I haven't figured out who that person is. Realistically, my go-to person for my panic attacks is Micha, but this time, it can't be him.

"Well, you have to tell me when you get ready to tell him. We'll do something big and make it a surprise." She pulls into the driveway of her house, pushes the button on the visor, and the garage door creeps open. "But promise me you'll do it soon. It'll wear you down, carrying this secret."

"You know me too well," I say as I unbuckle my seat

belt. Once she gets the car parked in the garage and the engine is off, I reach over and give her an awkward hug. I've never been much of a hugger, but I need her to understand how much she means to me. "Thank you for coming with me."

"You're welcome." She wraps her arms around me, embracing me back as she laughs under her breath. "I have to say, though, for you to hug me, those hormones have got to be intense."

Shaking my head, I lean back in the seat and laugh with her. It seems absolutely impossible with how terrified I am on the inside and makes me aware of just how lucky I am, even with life's curveballs.

Chapter 6
Micha

"What are you doing?" Ella startles me as she appears in the foyer without so much as making a sound.

"What are you, part ninja or something?" I ask as I drop the box of twinkle lights that I was carrying. "I didn't even hear you come in."

"I came in through the garage." She peers inside the box then glances at me perplexedly. "Are we decorating this year?"

My eyes pass over her. "We can if you want, but these aren't for us."

"Then who are they for?" She appears normal on the outside. Well, except for the fact that she's wearing a tank top and shorts, and it's cold as balls outside. Her eyes, though... There's something different about them. But, I can't put my finger on exactly what.

I cross my arms and stare her down. "Someone."

She frowns. "What's with the 'tude, dude?"

I nonchalantly shrug. "Nothing. I just don't feel like telling you my secret."

Her bottom lip juts out into a full-on pout. She looks so

damn adorable I have to remind myself not to tell her anything until she fesses up to me about why she went to the doctor this morning with Lila.

"But you always tell me your secrets," she whines.

My phone vibrates from my pocket and I fish it out.

"Well, I guess I'm just not in a sharing mood right now." I glance at the text message.

Ethan: We're good. Sent her to the store.

Putting the phone away, I collect the box from the floor and dodge around Ella. "Now, if you want to tell me where you were this morning, then maybe I can spill the beans."

"I was at the doctor." She sets her purse on the end table and faces me. "I told you that this morning."

I maneuver the box to my side. "But why did you go with Lila?"

"How did you know I went with Lila?" she asks suspiciously.

I shrug as I turn the knob and open the door. "I noticed the car was in the garage, so I went next door, and sure enough, Lila's car was missing. Ethan told me he had no clue where you two went."

"That's because he doesn't," she mutters, biting on her nails.

Something's definitely up. She's nervous and twitchy and biting her nails. But, I know her well enough to realize that, until she wants to talk to me, she won't.

So I step outside. "When you're ready to talk about whatever it is you're keeping a secret from me, let me know. Now, if you'll excuse me, I have some stuff to not tell you, too." I throw a winning grin at her and then shut the door.

An hour later, I start to leave Ethan's backyard with an empty box in my hand. "Good luck," I call over my shoulder as I reach the fence.

"Thanks. I'm going to need it," he answers, sounding more nervous than I've ever heard him.

Even though I know I shouldn't, I laugh at him. "You'll be fine, just as long as you don't let your dumbass side take over your mouth." I lift the latch and push the gate open.

He flips me the bird as he stares down at the grass. "You're an asshole, you know that?"

"No. I'm just paying you back for all the shit you gave me over the years." I kick the gate shut behind me then walk down the fence line and up the driveway toward my house.

It's the middle of the afternoon, the sun high in the clear blue sky. It makes me sort of homesick for Star Grove and the snow that always covers the yards during Christmas time. But, all thoughts of being homesick evaporate as I enter my bedroom.

"So what do you think?" Ella asks with her hands on her hips.

The box falls from my hands. "I think..." I'm struck speechless as she stands in the center of the bed wearing nothing except a lacey bra, matching panties, and knee-high socks. My cock goes rock hard. "I love it when you get like this."

I enthusiastically cross the room, tugging my shirt over my head. Once I make it to the foot of the bed, I reach for her, but she skitters to the side.

I frown. "What are you doing?"

"This," she says with her fiery, cocky attitude, "is for that shit-eating smirk you threw at me when you walked out the door."

My cock gets so hard it actually hurts. "You always play so dirty."

"That's because you're easy to play." She crosses her arms underneath her chest, her cleavage nearly bursting from the bra. "Now tell me what was up with the twinkle lights."

"Your tits look fucking amazing in that bra." I dodge around her question, fixated by her chest. "I just want to grab them." When I step toward her, she inches away, putting herself closer to the closet. "Ella," I gripe, sucking my lip ring into my mouth. "It's been two months."

She wickedly grins at me. "Oh, I know, which is going to make me getting my way a hell of a lot easier."

I'm getting antsy, needy, and downright horny. I need to come up with a plan here because I refuse to give up my secret until she divulges hers; otherwise, she might never tell me.

I glance from left to right, as if I'm searching for something. Like I guessed, she tracks my gaze. When she's distracted, I lunge for her, catching her off guard.

"Micha!" she squeals as my arms circle around her. "This is cheating."

"Cheating?" I question as I pick her up and carry her toward the bed. "This whole game of yours is cheating."

I drop her down on the mattress and she laughs, unable to get mad at me. Her laughter silences, though, as I tear off her bra and cup her breasts.

"The bra was no fair," I whisper as I dip my head toward her lips.

"So you're really not going to tell me?" she asks in a breathy groan as I pinch a nipple.

"Tell you what?" I brush my lips against hers and then glance at the clock. "In four hours, I won't tell you, but I'll show you."

"Oh, yeah?" She grins as her hand travels down the front of my jeans and her fingers stroke my hard-on. "Whatever will we do for those four hours?"

Laughing, I shake my head. "I have at least ten ideas." Then I seal my lips to hers, kissing her fiercely, letting all my feelings for her pour out through that kiss: every second I've spent away from this house and her, every smile I've missed, every laugh I didn't get to hear.

Not anymore.

Never again.

Minutes later, our clothes are off, and I'm sinking deep inside her. Her warmth engulfs me, calms me, lets me know I made the right choice. I nip at her lips, feel the softness of her flesh, the heat of her body as I thrust into her. She cries out my name over and over again as her head falls back against the pillow. Her glazed eyes, the halo of hair around her head, the want burning in her expression; they create lyrics and poetry through my head. When she starts moving with me, arching her hips to meet mine, the sensation is too much, and my head empties of all thoughts.

"I love you," I whisper against her lips as I give one final thrust inside her.

She clutches onto me with everything she has in her. "I love you, too."

Chapter 7
Ella

I'll admit, using sex was a dirty move. But it doesn't matter, since it didn't work. I still got to have sex, though, more than once. By the fourth time, I feel too exhausted to move.

I lie down on the bed, sweaty, tired, and breathless. "I feel like I should be asleep." I look up at the clock. "But I want to stay awake so you'll tell me your secret."

He laughs at me as he pulls on his boxers then settles on the mattress beside me. "You only have about ten more minutes. Think you can make it?"

"Maybe." I yawn. "You should talk to me, though, just to make sure I don't doze off."

He rolls to his side and props up on his elbow, staring down at me. "Well, I do have something... interesting to discuss with you."

I tense, wondering if he knows. How could he, though? The only people who know I'm pregnant are the doctor and Lila, and she swore not to tell.

"Relax." He traces my bottom lip with his finger. "It's not a bad thing. It's really good. At least, I hope you see it

71

that way."

I free a trapped breath. "Okay, lay it on me."

He appears nervous as he withdraws his finger from my lips. "Well, I quit the label."

My eyes pop wide. "What? When?"

He shrugs then sits up in the bed and reclines against the headboard. "I talked to Mike the last night you visited me on the road. My contract was coming to an end, anyway, and I just couldn't stand stuff anymore. The image change. The pressure." His gaze locks with mine. "Being away from you all the time."

I offer him a tentative smile as I move to sit up beside him. "So, what are you going to do?"

"I think I'm going to go Indie for a while." He stares over my shoulder at the sun descending in the sky, casting a shadow across the land. "I know some people that understand the Indie world, and I'm supposed to talk to them tomorrow. What I really want to do one day, though, is open my own studio." When his eyes meet mine again, he looks absolutely scared. "I know it makes our future a little iffy, but I promise you that, no matter what, I'll still take care of you. And I'll be here way more."

"Micha, if you're talking about money, we'll be fine." I glance around at our spacious home that we own. "We've earned more than we'll ever need. Plus, I have the art gallery."

"I know, but I'm still going to take care of you." He cups my cheek, and I lean against his palm, embracing his touch. "So, you're not mad?"

"Of course I'm not mad. Like I said, you've taken way better care of me than you ever needed to, and I love the idea of you being home more. I just want you to be happy."

He smiles at me. "I am happy. I just want to make sure you are."

I suck in a discreet breath and nod. "I am."

"Good." Suddenly, his gaze darts to the windows. "And happiness is about to spread even more."

"Why?" I start to turn my head to see what he's staring at, yet he grabs my hand and pulls me from the bed, guiding me toward the window and out onto the patio.

Wrapping the sheet around my body, I follow him outside, and then my jaw nearly drops to the ground.

Sparkling across the back lawn of Lila and Ethan's home is over a thousand white, twinkling lights that spell out *Will You Marry Me?* And standing next to the words is a very fidgety looking Ethan, decked out in a nice suit.

"That's what you two were doing?" I peer up a Micha. "You could have told me. I wouldn't have said anything to

Lila."

He shakes his head. "No way. I needed the secret for collateral, which, FYI, you still owe me a secret."

I force a tense smile, but before I can say anything, he holds up a finger. "Wait for it."

Moments later, the most delighted scream I've ever heard rings across the neighborhood.

"Oh, my God! Yes! Yes!" Lila cries, her voice getting louder and louder.

Micha and I are laughing as we lock eyes. But, his humor quickly vanishes.

"Remember when you said yes?" He tangles his fingers with mine and grazes his thumb across my ring. Only love fills his eyes, and it makes me feel wonderfully full.

"Of course." As my guilt surfaces, I place my arm across my stomach. "It was one of the best days of my life."

He gives me the most genuine smile then moves in to kiss me. When our lips connect, my guilt consumes me. I want to tell him, but I almost start to cry just thinking about what's happening to me. Realizing how brutal and ugly the words would be if they poured out of me right now, I decide to keep my lips sealed, not wanting to ruin his happiness.

When I can be happy myself, then I'll tell him.

Chapter 8
Ella

I manage to keep the secret for almost two weeks. It's not easy by any means, and I keep having a dream that I'm holding a little girl in my arms. On the thirteenth night of my secret keeping, though, I have the most terrible nightmare about the past and the day I ran out on Micha.

As I lie awake in bed the next morning after Micha has left to go search for a new studio, my guilt gnaws at me.

I need to tell him.

But, I need to be able to tell him without losing my shit.

I close my eyes and inhale and exhale like I was taught to do in therapy. Then I drag my ass out of bed and make the call I should have made two weeks ago when I got the news.

"Ella!" my sister-in-law Caroline cries as she answers the phone over the sound of cheery music. "I was just thinking about you."

"Really?" I pull on a pair of shorts with one hand before I head downstairs to find something to eat.

"Yeah, it was so weird, but I had a dream about you

last night," she says. "It must have been a sign that you were going to call me."

"I call you, like, once a week." I enter the kitchen and throw open the fridge, rummaging for something that looks tasty. I haven't gone shopping in a couple of weeks—too busy—so there's nothing in it that looks remotely good.

"But never this early," she says, and then the music silences. "Why aren't you at work?"

I close the fridge door. "I've been letting Gena run the place for the last couple of days."

"Why? I thought you said she couldn't handle it."

"She can't, but I've been... sick."

"Oh, my God!" she exclaims. "You're pregnant!"

My lips part in shock as I sink into a chair at the kitchen table. "How does everyone seem to know this when all I say is I'm sick. *I* didn't even jump right to that conclusion."

"You are twenty-five, Ella, and have been married for five years, so it was bound to happen soon. Plus, you have a glow in your voice."

I pick up an apple from a bowl on the table and scrunch my nose at the brown spots on it. "You can't hear a glow, Caroline."

"Yes, you can. But you're losing your glow right now, so what's up?"

I drop the apple back into the bowl and sigh. "It's nothing... I'm just... confused about this whole mother thing."

"That's understandable. I'm sure it has to be hard for you, especially with what happened to your mother."

"But it's not just that."

"What is it, then?"

I'm reluctant to answer, but it is the reason I called, so... "You know what our mother and father were like growing up, right? Dean's told you all about it, I'm assuming."

"Yeah, he's told me quite a bit. I've had to help him through some rough times." She hesitates. "Is that why you sound upset? Are you worried about what kind of parent you'll be?"

I nod as I whisper, "Yes... And I don't..." I suck in a deep breath as tears bubble in the corner of my eyes. "I don't know what to do."

Silence stretches between us. Since no one can see me, I let the tears fall freely.

"Don't tell him I told you this," Caroline says softly, "but Dean actually had to go to the emergency room when he first found out I was pregnant. He had such a bad panic attack he could barely breathe."

"What happened?"

"Nothing, really. The doctors gave him a sedative and sent us home."

"And then he was fine?" I've had enough panic attacks that I'm not buying it.

"Well, it took him some time, but then he got over it. I mean, you've seen him with Scarlett, Ella. He's a fantastic father, just like you're a fantastic aunt and will be a fantastic mother. Trust me, I've met some shitty parents who had the most fantastic mother and father growing up. It's all about the person you grew into, and you are an amazing person who's overcome a lot."

"You sound like a mom," I remark, amazed at how much freer I can breathe. Yeah, I'm still scared as shit, but it's not eating away at me so much at the moment. I'm able to wipe the tears away, and my eyes remain dry.

"That's because I am one to Scarlett and, soon, to this little one in my stomach." She pauses. "And I'll be there for you. Whatever you need, day or night, you call me. I don't have sisters I'm close with, so I need to hand my pregnancy knowledge to someone."

"Well, I'm going to need a lot of it." I push back from the table. "Thanks for this, Caroline. This helped a lot."

"Good, I'm glad." Silence draws out between us again.

"Ella, what does Micha have to say about all this? Considering how much he dotes over Scarlett, I'm betting he was really happy to hear the news."

Guilt crushes against my chest, like it has for the last couple of weeks. "I actually haven't told him about it."

"What! How long have you known?"

"Almost two weeks."

"Is he home?"

"Yeah."

"Ella." She sighs. "Go tell him. Right now. He deserves to know."

"I know he does." Leaving the kitchen, I march for the front door. "I just wanted to make sure I wasn't super upset when I told him. He's had to put up with me being really unstable during a lot of important moments, like when he proposed, said I love you, and right before we got married. I want, just for once, to tell him some life-changing news and be happy about it."

"And are you happy now?" she asks as I'm reaching for the doorknob.

I dither, contemplating while I attempt to sort through my emotions, something that's never an easy task. "I'm not sure if I'm happy yet, but it feels like I could get there. And I want to tell him."

"Good. Call me tonight and tell me how it goes."

"All right. I will," I promise.

We say good-bye and hang up, and then I hurry outside and over to Lila's house, not bothering to put any shoes on, way too nervous to even care.

"Are you nuts?" Lila says when she answers the door and notices my bare feet. "Ella, you're going to freeze to death before this pregnancy is over."

"I'll be fine." I squeeze by her and scurry into the house, doing a little dance on the carpet because the concrete did freeze the crap out of my feet on the way over here. I stop dancing, though, when I catch a whiff of the air. "Do I smell pancakes?"

Rolling her eyes, she closes the door then signals for me to follow her as she heads for the kitchen. "I think I should open my own restaurant or something with the way everyone acts around my food."

I grab a plate from the cupboard and a fork from the drawer as she picks up a platter of buttermilk pancakes from beside the griddle.

"You totally should, as long as I get to eat there all the time." I take a seat at the table while she collects the syrup from the fridge.

"You know what's funny?" She sets the platter down

on the table. "I never knew how to cook until a few years ago." She drops down in a chair and places the syrup in front of me. "While I was growing up, we always had a cook on hand, and when I left home, I just ate out all the time."

"I remember," I tell her as I stab a pancake with my fork and put it on my plate. "You wouldn't even clean up after yourself." I glance around at her sparkling counters and shiny stainless steel appliances. "But you have the hang of it now."

"That's because of Ethan." She looks down at the diamond ring on her finger, pink and sparkly, totally her. "He taught me how to take care of myself without falling apart."

"You guys are good together," I say, for some stupid reason feeling as though I'm going to cry. Before the waterworks spring free, I douse my pancakes with syrup and dive in.

"So, have you guys set a date yet?"

"February fourteenth." She beams.

"Valentine's day. Very you."

"The day was actually Ethan's suggestion."

"You know, sometimes I wonder if the asshole side he shows everyone else is just a façade." I wait for her to crack and tell me I'm correct.

She simply shrugs.

I cut my pancakes. "You know, I have to admit, I'm kind of sad."

Her forehead creases. "Over what?"

I shrug as I take a bite. "Well, I was really looking forward to you and Chester the cat living in the guestroom."

She laughs. "Sorry, but I was so not looking forward to that." She reaches for a pancake herself. "But enough talk about me. Let's talk about you."

I stuff my mouth full of pancakes. "What do you want to talk about?"

She gives me a warning stare. "How about you telling Micha that you're carrying his child. Seriously, Ella, it's almost been two weeks. Even I'm starting to go crazy keeping the secret."

"Yeah, sorry about that." Sighing, I set the fork down. "Actually, that's kind of why I came over, to have you give me some ideas on how to tell him."

She eyes the stack of pancakes in front of me. "And to eat my food."

I innocently shrug. "I can't help it if your food's delicious."

She rolls her eyes, yet her expression fills with joy.

"You're really going to tell him?"

I force down the lump in my throat. "Yeah, I think I'm ready."

She smiles cheerfully as she rises from the chair. "Good, because I have the perfect idea. But it's going to be intense."

Chapter 9

Ella

Later that afternoon, I stand in my studio. The air smells like fresh paint and promise. One of Micha's songs plays from my iPod dock, and my heart dances to the rhythm as I sing the lyrics under my breath.

The ghost of your soul still thrives.

Deep in your eyes yet buried alive.

Ashes surround you, drown you in pain.

A memory begging to drive you insane.

Haunting your soul, scorching your veins.

Yet heart and desire fights to enflame.

The tempo of the guitar, drums, and violin are reckless, racing, alive, and escaping, exactly how I feel at this moment. I breathe life into my art as my hand moves wildly, my fingers gripping the handle of a paintbrush, tracing lines, shading shadows, splattering bright and deep colors of paint across the canvas. Sweat beads my skin with each stroke, sheer terror and excitement pulsating through my body as vibrantly as the sunlight sparkling right outside the window. Every movement, line, and angle I make means more to me than any other painting I've ever created. Lila was right when she said it was going to be intense.

I express my emotions through my artwork. Right now, tears pour out of my eyes. Not necessarily sad tears. Confused tears, yes—I feel so confused about everything. Terrified tears, of course—terror over being a mom. Terror as I remember when I read my mother's journal and realized how terrified she was of being a mother.

But, through all the mixed emotions, there's also a tiny hint of excitement hidden inside me. I didn't think I could feel that way, but I do.

When I finally finish staining the canvas with my soul, I step back and stare at the creation. I not only feel confusion, terror, and excitement, I feel my life changing forever.

Chapter 10

Micha

It's a few days before Christmas Eve, and I'm coming home from work late, something I'm not happy about, but I couldn't help it. I've been working really hard to get on my own feet and get my own studio running, which means sacrificing time with Ella. I hate that I have to do it and hate how sad she's been about it, even though she pretends not to be. She's been sad a lot the last couple of weeks, and it's starting to worry me. Although, on the positive side, at least I'm home every night to try to cheer her up.

On my way home, I decide to stop and pick up a bottle of wine to surprise her. Not just for Christmas, but because almost six years ago from today, I asked her to unofficially marry me.

After I leave the liquor store, I drive home yet pause before I turn into the driveway. Lights are strung up on the trim and a few strings have been hung up around the windows. The strangest part, though, is that there's a small inflatable Santa on the front lawn that looks like he's waving at me. It creeps the heck out of me.

Shuddering, I park the car in the garage. When I enter

the house, the smell of apple pie engulfs my nostrils. It's not like Ella to bake anything, so the fact that she's making a pie throws me off a little.

"Honey, I'm home," I jokingly call out, setting my guitar case down by the back door. I then slip my jacket off and hang it on the coat rack.

Wandering into the kitchen, I inhale the apple pie scent. Moments later, I start to laugh as I take in the sight of the mess Ella's made in the kitchen. Flour practically dusts every inch of the countertops, and bowls, spoons, and pans are piled up in the sink. Plus, the air smells the slightest bit smoky. It's like a tornado swept through the place and scattered all of our cooking supplies everywhere, and in the middle of it, right on the stove, it left a single apple pie, all golden and crispy.

"Hey, you." Ella unexpectedly hurries through the doorway, looking a little flushed. Her auburn hair is braided to the side, a black dress hugs her body, and her porcelain skin is dotted with fresh paint. She's wearing no makeup at all.

She's fucking perfect. I'm so glad I get to see her like this.

"I'm really starting to enjoy coming home every night," I tell her, crossing the kitchen, excited to touch her.

88

She wipes her hands on the side of her dress. "Me, too. You're home late, though. Is everything okay?"

"Everything's fine. I just spent a little bit longer than I wanted to looking for places." I slip my arm around her waist and pull her against me, burying my face into the crook of her neck. "Tomorrow, you should come with me."

"I might be able to do that. I have to go to the gallery for a couple of hours, but we could meet up afterwards." She hooks her arms around me, and her fingers tremble as she traces the nape of my neck.

"Are you feeling better yet?" I dare ask. Every time I ask Ella about being sad or sick, she gets all twitchy.

She wavers, biting on her bottom lip. "Kind of."

"Maybe you should chill on the baking and take it easy."

She shakes her head. "Nah, I'm fine. Or, at least, I'm going to be." She contemplates something. "Did you like the decorations outside?"

"I did. Although, the Santa kind of creeped me out. Reminds me of that time when we were kids and I got stuck under the inflatable Santa when we were trying to deflate the one in front of the store."

She giggles, the warmth of her breath tickling my cheeks. "Ethan put it up just because of that."

89

"What a douche. I so need to get him back." I slide my hands down her body and cup her ass. "But later. Right now, I want something else." I grip her ass cheeks and push her closer to me, smiling when her eyelids flutter and her knees start to buckle.

"Later," she whispers in an unsteady voice. "Right now, I need to give you something."

I perk up. "Like a present?"

She nods. "But don't get too excited. It's nothing I bought or anything." When her voice gets all off-pitch, she clears her throat. "Just something we—I made."

Her offish behavior is a little weird, even for her, but I still play along.

"Awe, you made me a present." I wink at her. "How very sweet of you."

She laughs nervously, and I kiss her, pressing my hand against the small of her back. She whole-heartedly kisses me back, pushing her chest against me, as if she can't get enough.

We stay that way for a while but finally have to break apart to come up for air.

I lift up the wine I'm carrying. "How about we pour a glass of this, and then you can show me the present. I bought this to pre-celebrate our ring anniversary."

She glances down at the black-stone ring on her finger and then warily stares at the bottle of wine. "How about I show you the present first?"

"Okay...?" I'm having trouble reading her, which is unusual. My confusion only amplifies as she takes my hand, and I notice her fingers are trembling.

Still, I follow her as she guides me out of the kitchen and upstairs to her art studio. The space is equally as messy as the kitchen. Paint supplies, pencils, and canvases are everywhere, and the air smells of fresh paint. The lamp in the corner is on, but the shade is off and on the floor. There are also a few scraps of torn wrapping paper piled about and tape stuck to the hardwood floor.

Before I can say anything, she releases my hand and slowly walks over to the corner of the room where a present shaped an awfully lot like a canvas is propped against the wall.

"Okay, this present comes with warnings," she says, crossing her arms as she faces me.

I cautiously cross the room toward her. "And what warnings are those?"

"Well, the first is that Lila was actually behind the present idea, so I'm blaming any cheesiness factor on her. And the pie ordeal. She said I should bake for you as part of the

surprise, even though I told her I'd end up burning the pie."
She pauses, rubbing her hand across her face anxiously.
"And the second is that I'm not really sure if this"—she
waves her hand at the wrapped object—"is a present or
not." She frowns as she stares off into empty space. "I'm
still trying to figure it out."

She's got me fucking worried, but I attempt to remain
calm as I reach her. "Can I open it?"

Her chest rises and falls as she breathes in and out.
Then her gaze collides with mine. She doesn't utter a word,
just nods.

I reach out to rip the paper off. "I feel so nervous," I
admit as my fingers brush across the paper.

"I feel like I'm going to throw up," she mutters quietly.

My heart is hammering in my chest and blood rushes
in my eardrums. I'm so freaking worried I seriously expect
to find an '*I'm Divorcing You*' painted on the canvas hidden behind the green and gold paper. But, as I rip the paper
off, I discover a canvas painted with a very intriguing map.
Well, not necessarily a map, but a row of images that make
up a map of our lives together.

"It tells you a story," she whispers, watching me as I
study the painting. "A story that leads to an infinitely and
always ending, I hope."

I feel a shift in the air as my gaze skims across the map. The first image is of her and me standing on opposite sides of the fence when we're four years old. Then the paint brightens and alters in deeper colors as it creates our first kiss on a swing set when we were fourteen. Then the shades darken to greys, blacks, and charcoals as the scene transforms into us kissing on the bridge in the rain that night that changed our lives forever. After that, the lines sweep up and brighten at the replay of our wedding day in the snow, in our spot on the shore of the lake. I smile at that one, basking in the emotions connected to one of the best memories of my life. Finally, I arrive the end, but as soon as I see it, it doesn't feel like an end. It feels like a beginning.

My expression falters at the soft colors created with delicacy, as if each stroke of the brush meant something. The picture is of Ella and me in front of our house, but we're not alone. Standing between us is a little girl with red hair like Ella's and aqua eyes the same shade as mine.

"I don't know if it's going to be a girl," she says quietly as I stare at the painting in astonishment. "In fact, I was originally going to paint a boy, but when I actually started to paint it, it came out a girl, probably because I keep dreaming it's going to be a girl."

That's when what she's telling me *really* clicks.

I turn my head and look at her with uncertainty. Not because of my own feelings, but because I fear what's going on with her. She's been so afraid of being a mother, and I'm not sure if she's happy, sad, scared, or what.

"This is…" I trail off, clearing my throat. "When did this happen?"

She blows out an uneven breath. "Remember that night about two months ago on the piano? Well, I got a little off whack with my pills, and we got so caught in the moment I sort of forgot." Her chest heaves as she struggles to breathe. "I've known for a couple of weeks. That's why Lila went to the doctor with me that day, to find out for sure. Sorry I didn't tell you sooner. I was just freaking out that I'd be too sad and ruin everything for you."

"But you don't seem sad now." Anxious, yes. Scared, sure. Sad, not really.

She shrugs. "I'm coming to terms with it… Caroline kind of helped me this morning with a few things."

I swallow the lump in my throat. "So, you're for sure… pregnant?"

She swiftly nods. "Lila thought it'd be fun if I told you in some way special, so we came up with the painting idea." She fidgets with the hem of her dress. "I'm not so sure now that it was a good idea, springing it on you like this. You look… a little pale."

"I feel a little pale, but only because I'm trying to read you. I mean, we've talked about this enough that I was seriously starting to wonder if you'd ever be okay with having kids. And then it accidentally happened…" I trail off as I battle down my excitement. The last thing I want to do is celebrate if she's not ready for that.

"I'll be fine, Micha," she assures me, tangling her fingers with mine. "I'm not going to lie; I freaked the fuck out when Lila first suggested it to me. But, the more time goes by, the more… I don't know… I could see myself getting really into this."

Smashing my lips together, I press back a smile, not wanting to get too excited until I know that she's one-hundred percent okay with this. "Are you sure you're good with this? Because you can always tell me how you feel. You know that, right?"

She nods. "I do. And I'm not going to lie; I'm still scared as hell, but the idea of this"—she gestures at the last image on the canvas—"it makes me feel kind of bubbly inside sometimes when I think about it."

I let my smile slip through. "Good, because it makes me really, *really* happy."

"Are you sure?"

"Of course. I mean, I'm terrified as shit, but in a good, nervous, scared sort of way."

When she smiles, I scoop her up in my arms and hug her tightly.

"Best Christmas present ever," I say then press my lips to hers.

Chapter 11

A little less than two months later...

Ella

As I stand in front of the alter, waiting for the minister to pronounce Ethan and Lila husband and wife, all I can think is, *my feet hurt so bad.*

At a little over four months pregnant, heels were not the best choice of footwear. But, I love Lila enough that I'm trying to be a good sport and suck it up. Besides, she did have to go to over five stores to find the perfect bridesmaid's dress that would fit over my little belly.

To endure the pain, I focus on the best man standing across from me, looking smoking hot in a black tux. I never really thought a tux could be sexy, but I'll admit, I think my mind was changed today.

When Micha catches me checking him out, he winks at me. My stomach flutters with butterflies as I think about the time we stood up in front of our friends and swore our love for each other.

Lila and Ethan decided to keep it pretty simple—well, simple for Lila. There are maybe fifty guests tops, consisting of her friends and family. She didn't invite her mother or father and seemed pretty content about that. Ethan's family did show up, though, which is a little surprising.

Lila's dress, on the other hand, is anything other than simple. The silk and lace trails down half the aisle, and the corset top is embellished with flowers and diamonds that weave around her waistline. Her blonde hair is pinned up and curled, and a tiara glitters from the top of her head.

"And I now pronounce you husband and wife," the minster announces, drawing my attention back to the ceremony. "You may now kiss the bride."

Ethan and Lila lean in for a kiss, giggling under their breaths, which makes me giggle and Micha laugh. Lila glances at me perplexedly when she notices my laughter. I simply shrug then point to my stomach, blaming it on my hormones.

Shaking her head, she grins then links arms with Ethan and heads down the aisle. Micha and I do the same, following them, but unlike Ethan, Micha reaches behind me and sneakily pinches my ass.

I snort a laugh, although thankfully, we're out of the chapel and in the hallway by then.

"Not fair." I pinch Micha's ass back.

He laughs, wiggling his arm out of mine so he can skitter out of my reach. "That was way harder than mine."

Lila sets her bouquet of roses down and places her hands on her hips. "You two are relentless. Seriously, it's my wedding day. Can't you just chill for like a couple of hours and stop fondling each other?"

Micha and I exchange a wary look. "Maybe," we say simultaneously then sputter a laugh.

Ethan steps up to the side of Lila and swings his arm around her. "Relax, wife." The word causes a grin to spread across Lila's face.

Moments later, Ethan pinches her ass then bolts out the door toward the limo parked outside.

"Oh, he's so dead for that." She marches after him, the train of her dress swishing behind her.

Micha and I take hands and follow them out, getting into the limo that will drive us to the reception. On the way there, Ethan pops open a bottle of champagne to celebrate. He pours everyone a glass except for me. As if he's planned it, he reaches into his jacket pocket and retrieves a juice box.

When he offers it to me, I take it. "Did you seriously carry this around in your pocket the entire day?"

He shrugs. "I wanted to make sure you didn't feel left out."

I roll my eyes. "Oh, you did not."

"I did, too." He presses his hand to his chest, offended. "I'm being genuine right now. I promise." When I arch a brow at him, a conniving grin curls at his lips. "Okay, I'll admit, I thought it'd be funny to make you drink out of a juice box while the rest of us get to sip champagne. Call it payback for that stupid prank you pulled on me the other day."

Squaring my shoulders, I stab the straw into the top of the drink and take a sip as dignified as one can when drinking from a juice box. Micha chuckles under his breath then raises his glass.

"Okay, I have to make a toast. To the bride and groom, who are two of the best people I've ever met. I'm so glad they finally got married"—he pauses—"because it was about damn time."

Ethan rolls his eyes as the three of them clink glasses, and just so I won't feel left out, I tap my juice box against their glasses. By the time the champagne is finished, we've arrived at the reception hall.

"Are you ready to play?" Ethan asks as he grabs his drumsticks from the floor.

Micha nods as he pushes open the door. "But, just so you know, I'm not planning on making it a habit of jamming out at wedding receptions. I'm only doing this because I love the two of you so much."

Ethan makes gagging noises as he hops out while Lila throws her arms around Micha's neck and hugs the living daylights out of him. "You're so wonderful, Micha," she says, on the verge of crying.

He moves the heavy amounts of fabric from her dress out of the way so he can hug her back. With a soft pat on the back, the two of them break apart, and then Ethan helps Lila and her dress out of the car.

Micha ducks outside and offers his hand to me. Taking it, I very ungracefully get myself out of the limo, trying not to flash anyone as my short green dress threatens to flip up.

"Have I told you lately how beautiful you are?" he asks as he shuts the door, still holding my hand.

I nod as we head for the door of the building. "In fact, I'm pretty sure you told me that just an hour ago when we were walking up the aisle."

He grins and drops a kiss on my mouth as we step inside the entryway. Then he lowers himself to his knees and places his hands on my stomach. The first time he did this in public, I got extremely uncomfortable and made him stop. But, now, it's growing on me, and I actually kind of find it sweet.

"You're going to be just as beautiful as your mother,"

he whispers to my bump. His fingers spread across my stomach, and he starts singing an unfamiliar song under his breath. "Words will never be able to describe how much I love you."

"What is that?" I ask, staring down at him. "Is that one of your new songs?"

He shrugs as he rises back to his feet. "I actually wrote it for her the other day when we found out it's a girl. I'm still working on it, though."

"What are you going to call the song?"

"I was thinking about calling it, 'Lyric.' " He tucks a strand of hair behind my ear. "And I was kind of thinking we could give her the same name."

I rest a hand on my belly. "You want to name our daughter Lyric?"

He shrugs. "It kind of seems fitting." His lips expand to an enormous grin. "I mean, she was created on a piano."

His smile is contagious, causing my own to take over my face. "You know what? I think Lyric sounds perfect."

Coming November 25, 2014

Unraveling You

(A new series starring Ella and Micha's daughter and Lila and Ethan's son)

Ella and Micha: Infinitely and Always

Enjoy a sneak peak at The Prelude of Ella and Micha

Now available!

Chapter 1

14 years old...

Ella

I trudge home from school an hour early with a dark, bluish-purple bruise splattered across my cheek, a thin cut across my bottom lip, and a pink detention slip inside my backpack. It's not the first time I've been sent home over a fight, and I'm sure it won't be my last. I have a knack for fights. Not because I'm a bully. In fact, I'm the polar opposite and tend to get into fights with the bullies whenever they're picking on someone. I'm not trying to be a hero or anything. I just have a vast dislike for people getting picked on. Plus, I like the rush that comes from jumping in and doing something instead of standing by and watching.

There are always consequences for my actions, although not usually from my parents. By the time I get home, my mother will probably be sedated from the intense meds she's on for her Bipolar Disorder. And my dad will either be at work or at the bar trying to drink away the fact that my mother has a mental illness. Neither of them will care about the condition of my face or the detention slip.

No, my ass is going to get reamed by Micha Scott, aka my best friend since forever. Aka my best friend who thinks I'm his responsibility for whatever reason.

I still have a couple of hours before school releases and he shows up at my house so when I arrive home, I decide to de-stress after chores. The first thing on my to-do list, though, is a painkiller to alleviate my headache.

Going into the kitchen, I drop my backpack on the table, grab a bottle from the medicine cabinet, and pop two pills into my mouth. Then I fetch some ice from the freezer and place it on my eye, holding it there while I hurry and pick up the week's worth of garbage littering the floor. Most of the contents that end up in the trash bag are empty bottles of vodka, tequila, and beer. I do find some stale takeout wedged between the fridge and the counter along with a few pots and pans on the table that are caked with month old grease. The fridge was open when I entered the kitchen, probably left that way by my mother. Thankfully, there's hardly any food inside that could have spoiled.

After I shut the fridge, I sort through the past due bills

I collected from the mailbox and try to figure out which ones to pay this week. Then I make out the checks, leaving the signature line blank for my dad to sign whenever he gets home. It's exhausting thinking about money, and the process makes me kind of regret getting sent home early.

So much for de-stressing.

Once the kitchen is polished and the checks are filled out, I lose the ice pack and peek in on my mom in her bedroom. She's sprawled out on the mattress, snoring, with her arm draped over the edge of the bed and a bottle of pills next to her. Tiptoeing to the bed, I pick up the bottle and count how many pills there are inside. Three less than from this morning, which means she's okay and hasn't taken too many.

Keeping track of the pills is something I've had to do for a couple of months now, ever since she accidentally took too many and ended up in the emergency room. After they pumped her stomach, the doctors and nurses put her on suicide watch for twenty-four hours, even though my mother insisted the overdose was accidental—that she'd forgotten she'd already taken her dose in the morning. The doctors didn't seem to believe her, but I do because there's no way she'd intentionally want to die. How could she? She's my mother.

I put the medicine bottle in the bathroom cabinet then leave the bedroom and wander into my room. The purple walls are freshly painted with black skulls thanks to Micha, who decided the other day that my room was too girly for him. It's cool, though. I dig the skulls. Plus, I'm not a girlie girl at all. My typical outfit is holey jeans and a dark T-shirt. Sometimes I wear a hoodie. I never wear makeup and almost always put my auburn hair up in a ponytail because doing anything else with it is a pain in the ass. Sneakers are my choice of footwear. Right now, the pair of shoes I'm wearing match my walls.

Collecting my sketch book and pencil from the dresser, I flop down on my bed and attempt to unwind by getting lost in my art. But, after a while, the silence of the house gets to me, so I turn on my stereo that's about twenty years old. I cruise the radio stations and choose a classic one because my only other options are country and heavy metal. Then I situate myself on my bed again and continue working on the sketch that's for my art class. A vase. So boring.

Finally, I decide to take a break and flip the page to one of my own projects, one of Micha that I will never, *ev-*

er show him, because it's embarrassing. I have no idea how he'd react if he knew I was drawing him, and I never want to find out. But I can't seem to stop—he's always stuck in my head.

Ten minutes later, my hand moves mindlessly across the crisp page, creating sharp angles, soft curves, dark shading. The portrait creation goes on for what seems like forever, and when I finally blink back to reality, I feel more content than I have all day.

Deciding to stop for now, I shake the cramp out of my hand and get up and stretch before cranking up the music. "We Got the Beat" by The Go-Go's blares through the speakers. I stand up on the bed and rock out, jumping up and down on the mattress and spinning in circles. Mid chorus, I tug the elastic from my hair and start head banging, really getting into the beat. If I was musically talented, I would so be a drummer or a singer, but art is my forte. Music is Micha's talent. He can play the guitar like a pro, and his voice is the most beautiful sound I've ever heard in all my fourteen years. Of course, I don't tell him this. He'd tease me and call me a silly girl if I divulged the sappy side of me.

As I'm in the middle of a very awesome air guitar solo, I notice a gentle breeze has fluttered into the room.

"Dammit," I curse, knowing what the chill means. What I don't know is whether it's better if I just continue dancing until maybe Micha leaves or stop and face the embarrassment. Then again, I really don't want him to leave, never do.

Pressing my lips together, I stop shaking and shimmying, plaster on my best smile, and turn on the bed to face him, trying to appear all sweet and innocent, like he didn't just catch me rocking out to 80s rock.

His tall, gangly figure lingers near the window, the place he always enters my room by climbing up the tree just outside. He's sporting black jeans and a matching T-shirt decorated with a red skull and crossbones, and his sandy blond hair is a little on the longish side, hanging across his forehead and in his eyes. Micha's eyes are actually super intense, a fierce aqua blue color, similar to the ocean.

"Hey." I casually wave, plopping down onto the mattress with a bounce. Then I lean over to turn the radio down.

His gaze instantly darts to the fresh shiner on my cheek

"Did you have fun today?" he asks, folding his arms and reclining against the wall as his stare bores into me.

I shrug, scratching my injured cheek. "You know how I love to dance."

He shakes his head, but his lips quirk, a smile threatening to slip through. "I'm not talking about the dancing." He stands up straight and crosses the room toward my bed. "I'm talking about you getting into a fight today with Diana Rollinson."

"Oh, that." I stand up and square my shoulders, hating that I have to tip my head back to look at him. It's not like I'm short or anything. Up until about three months ago, I was taller than him. But, almost overnight, he shot up and now has me by about six inches. "Look, I know you hate it when I get into fights, but Diana was being a bitch to Sandy, who barely says two words to anyone."

"So you were defending someone's honor. By getting punched in the face."

"Hey." I cross my arms and glare at him. "I got in quite a few swings before this thing happened." I point at the bruise on my cheek, "Which, FYI, came from when she pushed me into the lockers, not from her fists. She can't even punch, total hair puller."

He's struggling not to laugh while remaining my four-teen-year-old voice of reason, more mature for his age than most guys. "What about the cut on your lip?"

I elevate my hands in front of me and make scratching motions in the air. "She's a total clawer, too." I sigh when he continues to stare at me without so much as a tiny grin. "Look, I'm sorry, okay? But it's not that big of a deal. I only got sent home early today."

His head slants to the side as he gently brushes his finger across the tender area on my cheek. "You're going to ruin that pretty face of yours if you keep this up."

I stick out my tongue as my cheeks heat. I loathe compliments, even when they're meant sarcastically. "Ha, ha, you're a freaking riot, Micha Scott."

He presses his hand to his chest, giving me an innocent look. "I call you pretty, and you stick your tongue out at me? Seriously, Ella May, you just broke my heart."

And, just like that, the tension breaks after only a minute of chatting.

Always does.

Which is why I need Micha in my life.

Even if he tries to be my voice of reason.

"I'm sure I did," I retort sarcastically with an eye roll, which he seems to find more amusing than anything. "Okay, I'm sorry I got into a fight and got my *pretty*"—I roll my eyes again— "face ruined. But I won't promise that I'm not going to do it again, because I don't make promises I know I won't keep."

"One of these days, you're going to get into trouble." His gaze drifts over my shoulder to my bed. "You know that." His forehead creases as he studies something behind me.

I twist around to see what he's looking at and realize I left my sketchbook out on my bed, opened to the page displaying the detailed sketch of Micha sitting under a massive oak tree. His head is tipped down, he has a pen in his hand, and there's a notebook on his lap that he's scribbling lyrics into.

"Oh, shit." I leap for the bed and snatch it up, pressing the drawing to my chest.

"What was that?" he asks as I roll over on my back, hugging the book to my chest as I look up at him.

"Nothing," I say quickly, which is clearly a mistake.

He kneels down on the bed, putting a knee on each

side of me, like he does whenever we wrestle. "Come on, Ella May, let me see," he says in the sweet voice he only uses whenever he's trying to get his way.

"That voice doesn't work on me." I attempt to slide upwards on the bed and out from under him. "It only works on girls like Diana."

He chuckles, but doesn't budge, and I continue to wiggle, fighting to get out from underneath him.

"Come on. Let me go," I plead.

"Not until you let me see whatever it is you're hiding from me."

"No way." My grasp tightens on the book. "My drawings are private. You know that." Which is kind of a lie. Only drawings of him are private.

He considers what I've said then, with a sigh, he climbs off me. "Oh, fine. You win."

"I always win," I say, shooting him a cocky grin.

"Well, if you're going to act that way." He dives back on me and starts tickling me until I drop the sketchbook.

"You are the meanest boy ever!" I laugh so hard tears stream down my cheeks.

He grins as he releases me and backs up off the bed. The smile slips from his face as he catches sight of my sketchbook and the drawing I was trying to hide from him. His expression is unreadable—confused and kind of … flattered?

"You're drawing me?" He looks at me with curiosity written all over his face.

My cheeks erupt with heat as I flop back on the bed and stare up at the Chevelle poster on my ceiling. "I was bored, okay? The art class projects are too cliché, and I needed to work on improving my life drawings." *Liar, liar.*

I wait for him to call me out because he knows me well enough that he can.

He leans over and picks the sketchbook up off the floor. "You want to go to the park with me and hang out for a bit?" he asks as he tosses the book onto my dresser.

I prop up on my elbows and arch my eyebrows at him. "What? No snarky remarks about how my drawing means I'm secretly in love with you? Or that I think you're so dreamy?" I make a joking swoony face then gag.

He snorts a laugh then waves me off. "Nah, I don't need to repeat something we both already know." When I pinch his arm, he laughs. "Come on. Come to the park with me." He pouts out his lip. "Pretty please. It'll be fun."

I roll my eyes but easily give in, knowing he'll keep looking at me like that until I do. Besides, I'm never one to pass up the opportunity to get out of the house.

"Fine," I surrender, sitting up. "But only because I have nothing better to do."

Grinning like a goof, he offers me his hand and hauls me to my feet. He doesn't let go, slipping his fingers through mine as he leads me out of my room and down the stairs.

The holding hands gesture is nothing new. Ever since we became best friends ten years ago, he usually either has his arm around me, is holding my hand, tickling me, or touching my hair. Sometimes, I think he doesn't even realize he's doing it. Renee, this girl that I sometimes hang out with, thinks it's because Micha has a crush on me and is secretly in love with me. I laugh whenever she tells me this because Micha isn't in love with me, at least, not like the way she means it. He's already kissed like three girls, and I don't see him ever trying to kiss me. Well, except for maybe on the cheek.

"So how bad did Diana look after the fight?" Micha asks after we've exited my house and entered the neighborhood we've both grown up in. "I'm guessing you got her pretty good."

"Of course I did," I reply as we start up the sidewalk lined with rundown homes. It's late afternoon and most of the area appears like it's sleeping. But that's typical for Star Grove. Around ten is when the yards and houses will be flooding with loud noises of parties taking place. "Both her eyes were swollen."

He smiles then leans over and gives me a quick kiss on the head. Then we continue our journey down the sidewalk in comfortable silence. When we arrive at the desolate playground, we hike across the dry grass to the rusty swing set in the middle. We each sit down in our own seat and then run back and pump our legs, swinging high toward the tip of the nearby trees.

"Do you ever wonder what life would be like on the other side of the mountains?" I ask as I stare at the rolling hills that encompass the town.

"Of course I do." He kicks his legs, ascending higher as he tips his head back toward the grey sky.

"Do you think we'll ever get to find out?" I grasp the chains as I soar. "Do you ever think we'll get out of here?"

"Of course we will," he says. "There's no way we can

stay here in this stupid town forever."

"Yeah, but I'm not sure if I'll ever be able to leave my mother behind," I mutter. "I mean, who will take care of her if I'm not around? My dad's not capable of doing so, and Dean's not ever going to." Dean is my older brother who is probably home about twice a week, only coming back to change his clothes. I have no idea where he stays during the rest of the week.

"So what? They can figure that out." Micha's jaw is set tight, and his blue eyes burn fiercely. "You're not staying here. You're leaving with me."

"We'll see," I sigh. "At eighteen, we might not even be friends anymore. I've heard high school is rough."

He's silent for a while, contemplating what I've said. It's not like I really believe high school will ruin our friendship. I just don't believe I'll ever be able to leave Star Grove. It's just hope, and I've hoped for a lot of things I've never gotten.

Micha abruptly plants his feet into the dirt below us and skids to a halt. Without uttering a word, he reaches over and grabs the chain of my swing, causing me to jerk to a stop, spin around, and crash straight into him.

"Holy crap," I say breathlessly as I clutch onto the

chains. "What the heck did you do that for?"

"Because I want you to understand something," he says intensely. "You and I are going to leave this town. *Together*." He pauses when I stare at him with doubt. Then he thoughtfully adds, "In fact, we're going to make a pact on it. Right here. Right now."

"Haven't we made a ton of those already?"

"So what's one more?"

"Good point." Still, I'm a pessimist when it comes to ever escaping this town. Most people born and raised here never leave. But I'll try anything to boost the odds from not being a statistic. Plus, the future he's proposed doesn't sound all that bad. In fact, it sounds nice. "All right, let's make a pact."

He grins then spits into his palm before extending his hand toward me. "Ready?"

"You know, we really need to come up with a less disgusting way to make these pacts." But I still spit into my palm and place my hand in his.

"So who's going to say it this time?" he asks. "You or me?"

"I'll do the honors." I consider my word choice.

"Okay, so here's the deal. As soon as we turn eighteen, we rummage all our money together and get the hell out of here. No questions asked."

"And where will we live?" he asks amusedly.

I shrug. "How about by the ocean? We've never seen it before. It might be cool."

"The ocean sounds nice." He muses over something.

"Sounds good to me. Leave, go to the ocean. You can become a famous artist, and I'll become a musician."

"And we'll make sure we have better lives," I add. "Ones we're happy with."

"Agreed," he says and then we shake on it. "Although, I have to say that I'm not sad about everything in my life right now."

Unlike me, Micha has a stable parent—his mother who I sometimes like to pretend is my own mother when I'm having a rough day. Still, things haven't always been easy for him. His father walked out on Micha and his mom about eight years ago, and it was both financially and emotionally hard on them.

"I'm talking about you," Micha adds, letting go of my hand.

I blink my attention back to him. "What?"

He winks at me before walking back with his fingers wrapped around the chains. "You, Ella May, are the creation of my happiness." He lifts his legs and shoots forward.

I roll my eyes as I back up. "You are so stinking cheesy sometimes. No other fourteen-year-old boy talks the way you do."

"How do you know that?" he questions as he swings back and forth. "Are their more fourteen-year-old guys in your life that I don't know about?"

I shrug as I launch forward. "Ethan. And he doesn't talk like that."

"He might."

"Yeah, right."

"Hey, he's my best friend," he teases as we level out and swing harmoniously together. "For all you know, he could talk like that when you're not around."

I jut out my lip, pouting. "Hey, I thought I was your best friend."

"No way," he says in all seriousness. "You're way more than that."

I flop my head back, gagging. "God, stop with the cheesy pickup lines. It's making me nauseous."

"Fine, but only if you play truth with me."

"Fine, but only if I get to ask the first question."

He smiles. "Be my guest."

I contemplate. "So, Micha Scott, just how many girls have you kissed now?"

He suspiciously glances at me from the corner of his eye. "You already know the answer to that since you asked me the same question the last time we played this."

"Yeah, but it's been a few weeks since then." I lift my shoulder and give a half shrug. "And I heard a rumor yesterday."

"About what?"

"That you and Kessa kissed behind the school during third period."

He shoots me a dirty look. "Fuck no. I would never kiss Kessa Finlany. Who told you that?"

"Kessa."

He frowns, staring ahead at the playground. "Well, that never happened. And it will never happen."

"Noted." I swing higher, and he matches my move, stretching his legs toward the sky. "So the number is still three?"

"Yep, still three." He grows silent, his face contorting

in deep thought as he debates his question for me. When he arrives at his conclusion, a slow grin expands across his face, and I know I'm in big trouble. "So, Ella May, just how many boys have *you* kissed?"

The chilly breeze stings at my warm cheeks. "That's not a fair question."

"And why's that?"

"Because you already know the answer to that."

"And how do you figure that? I mean, for all I know, something could have changed since the last time I asked you."

"You know it hasn't," I say, feeling stupid. "I pretty much don't hang out with anyone but you."

His brow cocks and amusement dances in his eyes. "So the number's still zero?"

I grip the chains, annoyed. "See, you already knew the answer, so that wasn't a fair question."

"Why? It's my wasted turn." He sticks his feet to the ground again and this time grinds to a slow halt. Then he just sits there motionlessly as he watches me swing back and forth.

"What are you doing?" I wonder as I kick my feet

higher. Strands of my auburn hair slip lose from my pony-tail and surround my face. "Why are you looking at me like that?"

He muses over something, rubbing his jawline. "I have a proposition for you."

"No way," I instantly respond. "I know better than to agree to your propositions."

"Just hear me out first," he says, using the voice again. "Then you can make your decision."

Sighing, I plant my feet in the dirt to stop beside him, knowing he won't give up until I at least agree to hear whatever it is he's thinking. "Fine, what's your proposition?"

"I propose," he starts, seeming the slightest bit uneasy, which is weird for him, "that I be your first kiss."

I snort a big, old, pig laugh. "Ha, very funny. For a moment, I thought you were going to be serious."

"I am being serious." His expression matches his words.

And my expression plummets. "W-what? Why would you ever ask me that? Or want to do that?"

He shrugs. "You have to get your first kiss over some-time, so why not do it with me?"

125

I scrunch up my nose. "Because you're ... you." I don't mean for it to come out so rude. Luckily, Micha knows me well enough not to take it personally.

His lips quirk. "And what's wrong with me? Am I too hideous for you?"

"No," I sputter quickly, and he laughs. "That's not it at all. I'm just ..."

"You're just what, waiting around for the perfect guy to show up? Like Grantford Davis?"

"Ew." I swat his arm, and his laughter increases. "No way. I would never, *ever* use my first kiss on him. He's so weird and gross."

"A lot of the guys our age are weird and gross. Except me."

"That's not entirely true," I say then pause. "But I guess, out of all the guys at our school, you are the least gross."

"Okay, then," he states like this solves the problem. "Let's do this."

Do what?

Kiss Micha?

God, I've barely even hugged anyone, let alone kissed

126

anyone.

I should protest more—I know I should—but a part of me is curious as to why the hell kissing is such a big deal.

"You promise you won't make fun of me or anything?"

He gives me a *really* look. "Do I ever make fun of you?"

I throw back the look he just gave me. "All the time."

"But that's just for fun." He waves me off. "I don't mean any of it."

"Just promise me you won't tease me, and I'll do it. In fact, you have to promise not to ever bring it up." I spit into my hand. "Make a pact on it."

He considers my proposal for about a half a second then spits into his palm and shakes on it. "Deal."

As we pull our hands away, I grow nervous because now I have to actually kiss him. And not just kiss *him*, but kiss my first guy *ever*.

"Are you sure you want to do this?" I double check, wiping my palm on my jeans. "Because I don't know what I'm doing."

"I'll show you." He's already leaning in, his intense aqua eyes zeroed in on my lips.

My heart dances like a crazy person in my chest, and I feel like I'm going to throw up. "Micha, I …" I trail off, sucking in a huge breath as his lips touch mine. My fingers tense around the chains and my whole body stiffens while I try to figure out what on earth I'm supposed to be doing. Clearly not just sitting here, frozen.

"Relax," Micha whispers, putting a small bit of space between our lips.

Thinking the kiss is over, I let out a quiet, relieved breath. But the relief is short lived because, a microsecond later, his head dips forward and his lips brush against mine again. Only, this time, it's different. This time, he slips his tongue into my mouth.

Oh, my God, his tongue is in my mouth.

Micha Scott's *tongue is in my mouth.*

And I just touched my tongue to his.

Before I can even register what's happening, we're kissing. And I mean full on French-kissing. It goes on for what feels like minutes, our knees knocking against each other as Micha plays with my hair and continues to kiss me. Unfamiliar feelings prickle inside me, ones I'm pretty sure I've never felt before, and that terrifies the living daylights out of me. They make me feel so...

Out of control.

And Micha is supposed to be my stability.

I'm about to pull away because I can't take the terror hounding inside me anymore when a loud crash echoes from nearby and we both jerk apart, wide-eyed and gasping for air. My cheeks start to burn and even Micha appears embarrassed, which has never happened before—at least, from what I've seen.

Seconds later, reality crashes over me.

Oh, my God, I just kissed my best friend.

The silence that follows is painful, and I worry that everything is going to change. Be ruined. He won't want to be my friend anymore, and if I don't have him, I have no one.

I wish I never kissed him.

"Well, that was interesting," Micha remarks, touching his fingers to his lips as he chuckles.

"Interesting, as in bad?" I ask, nervous for unclear reasons.

He swiftly shakes his head. "No way. Not bad at all." That's all he says before he runs back and starts swinging again. "So, did you hear that Ethan and Jane are going out?"

Confused by the abrupt subject change, I slowly let the swing crawl forward. "No."

"Yeah, he told me the other day." He starts chatting about who's going out with who, updating me on the latest middle school gossip, but I zone out, my thoughts floating back to the kiss.

It felt so right yet so wrong. So good yet so terrifying. Are things going to change after this? Do I look as awkward as I feel on the inside? What is happening to me? Micha usually calms me down, but right now, being close to him is freaking me out. Although, in a good way, a way I don't know how to handle.

As my thoughts and emotions start to jumble together, I feel like a huge mess. Finally, I arrive at a conclusion: never again. Never will I kiss Micha again.

Never, ever will I risk our friendship and our beautiful future together again

Jessica Sorensen

About the Author

Jessica Sorensen is a *New York Times* and *USA Today* bestselling author that lives in the snowy mountains of Wyoming. When she's not writing, she spends her time reading and hanging out with her family.

Other books by Jessica Sorensen:

<u>The Coincidence Series:</u>

The Coincidence of Callie and Kayden

The Redemption of Callie and Kayden

The Destiny of Violet and Luke

The Probabilty of Violet and Luke

The Certainty of Violet and Luke

The Resolution of Callie and Kayden

Unbeautiful (Coming Soon)

Seth & Grayson (Coming Soon)

The Secret Series:

The Prelude of Ella and Micha

The Secret of Ella and Micha

The Forever of Ella and Micha

The Temptation of Lila and Ethan

The Ever After of Ella and Micha

Lila and Ethan: Forever and Always

Ella and Micha: Infinitely and Always

The Shattered Promises Series:

Shattered Promises

Fractured Souls

Unbroken

Broken Visions

Scattered Ashes (Coming Soon)

Breaking Nova Series:

Breaking Nova

Saving Quinton

Delilah: The Making of Red

Nova and Quinton: No Regrets

Tristan: Finding Hope

Wreck Me (Coming Soon)

The Fallen Star Series (YA):

The Fallen Star

The Underworld

The Vision

The Promise

The Fallen Souls Series (spin off from The Fallen Star):

The Lost Soul

The Evanescence

The Darkness Falls Series:

Darkness Falls

Darkness Breaks

Darkness Fades

The Death Collectors Series (NA and YA):

Ember X and Ember

Cinder X and Cinder

Spark X and Cinder (Coming Soon)

The Sins Series:

Seduction & Temptation

Sins & Secrets

Lies & Betrayal (Coming Soon)

Standalones

The Forgotten Girl

<u>Coming Soon:</u>

Unraveling You

Entranced

Steel & Bones

Connect with me online:

jessicasorensen.com

http://www.facebook.com/pages/Jessica-Sorensen/165335743524509

https://twitter.com/#!/jessFallenStar

Ella and Micha: Infinitely and Always

Made in the USA
Lexington, KY
03 April 2017